"Let me help."

His hands took the key from hers and he slid it into the lock with careful deliberation. But it wasn't the key that had Julia's attention. It was the feel of his leather jacket beneath her cheek…the scent of sawdust…the rugged shoulders, sheltering her from the late-winter wind.

Hope stole over her. She tried to fight the emotion, but couldn't. It began in his gentle, strong manner and was nurtured by his serious gaze and his bright smile. He'd seemed downright prickly last week, but she saw none of that now.

But you did see it, so don't be fooled. People aren't always what they seem.

The key turned easily when Tanner tugged the door their way. He finished locking it, dropped the key into her hand, then tipped his gaze down from over her shoulder. "We're good."

His words reminded her of old dreams, gone awry. A home, filled with children and a set of loving parents. Was she shortsighted to think the dream could still exist?

Multipublished, bestselling author **Ruth Logan Herne** loves God, her country, her family, dogs, chocolate and coffee! Married to a very patient man, she lives in an old farmhouse in upstate New York and thinks possums should leave the cat food alone and snakes should always live outside. There are no exceptions to either rule! Visit Ruthy at ruthloganherne.com.

Books by Ruth Logan Herne

Love Inspired

Kirkwood Lake

Men of Allegany County

Big Sky Centennial

Visit the Author Profile page at Harlequin.com for more titles.

Healing the Lawman's Heart

Ruth Logan Herne

HARLEQUIN® LOVE INSPIRED®

Recycling programs
for this product may
not exist in your area.

™ LOVE INSPIRED BOOKS

ISBN-13: 978-0-373-81843-3

Healing the Lawman's Heart

www.Harlequin.com

Printed in U.S.A.

And I will betroth you to me forever. I will betroth you to me in righteousness and in justice, in steadfast love and in mercy.
—*Hosea* 2:19

To Angela and Kim, two amazing and
wonderful women... God is good all the time.
Men, on the other hand, are a work in progress.
And to all who've kissed a sweet child's brow
goodbye too soon... May God hold you
in the palm of His hand as you heal.

Chapter One

New York state trooper Tanner Redding-ton scanned the sketchy neighborhood with a practiced eye. All was calm at present, but after a dozen years on the force, Tanner was no stranger to life's quick changes.

A winter storm warning had advised local businesses to shut down for the day. Most had heeded the warning, but scattered bright windows said not everyone had closed up, despite the harsh conditions about to descend on Western New York.

Typical, thought Tanner as he sipped his coffee. When he burned his tongue, he scolded himself and pushed to keep his mind on his work. Normally, that wasn't a big deal. Tanner lived his job.

But with the first days of March looming? The next few days were always tough, a face-to-face reckoning with anniversaries he couldn't forget. And then the calendar mercifully flipped and time moved on.

Lights shut off south of him as a short stretch of shops called it a day.

There were always a few that stayed open till the last possible moment, then made a bad situation worse by trying to get home in rough winter conditions. Today's storm would be no exception, but as he scanned the interstate entrance to his left, the low volume of traffic said a lot of folks had paid attention this time.

His peripheral vision caught something out of place. He swiveled in the driver's seat, sure he'd seen a blink of light that hadn't been there minutes before. He scanned the thin gray light of late afternoon to determine what he saw.

Nothing seemed out of place.

Focused, he set his coffee down and studied a group of buildings just south of the above-grade interstate entrance.

Another blink of light pinpointed the action. But what was it? And why was it coming from that vacant building?

He put the cruiser into Drive and headed toward the decrepit structure. Other than a long-established shoe shop run by an eccentric but knowledgeable distance runner, the neglected strip mall had sat empty for several years.

Cops hated empty buildings. Empty buildings offered shelter for shady characters and an opportunity for foolish kids to create trouble. This scruffy stretch of decay had been slated for demolition twice. Both times, legal mumbo jumbo got in the way. Last he heard, some do-gooder had bought it for back taxes, promising the world.

That was months ago, and so far, nothing had changed. Tanner reported his location and his intention, knew backup was on the way, and slipped into the parking lot at the far end by the shoe store.

A lone car sat parked in front of the north-facing vacant building. He ran the plate and came up with the name of a rental car agency.

Which meant whoever was inside didn't want to be traced.

Trooper Zach Harrison pulled up alongside Tanner less than two minutes later. "What have we got?"

"That." Tanner pointed toward the messed-up building and just as he did, the bob of light shone from inside again.

"Car?" Zach jutted his chin toward the late model Chevy standing alone outside the building.

"Rented."

"Of course."

Tanner pulled his cruiser around to the front, tucked it into the corner and climbed out. Zach followed suit.

As they drew close to the ratty storefront on the end, Tanner put his hand over his weapon, ready to defend himself. He nodded to Zach.

Zach took flank and Tanner rapped hard on the door.

The light flicked off, plunging the interior into darkness.

"New York State Troopers. Open up!"

Nothing.

Which meant whoever was inside was either scared…or dangerous. Tanner tried the door.

Locked.

He motioned to Zach.

Zach nodded, started to move forward, then paused. He reached into his pocket, withdrew his phone, dropped his head back and sighed. "Julia, it's me. Get out here. Now."

The light blinked on inside, and this time it stayed on.

A key turned in the lock of the scuffed-up door. Tanner took a step back as the door swung his way.

Julia—whoever she was—stepped out.

Beautiful.

Blond hair pinned up, great eyes, glasses tucked up into the hair and a look on her face that said she might be ready to kill someone. "You big lug. You scared me to death. What's the matter with you, coming looking for me like this? Is everything all right? Are the boys okay? Is it Dad? Or Jackson?" She clamped a hand on Zach's arm with a grip that said she wasn't afraid to take care of herself. "What's happened, Zach?"

"Him."

She turned Tanner's way as if just noticing him. "You?"

"The light." Tanner motioned toward the building interior. "You were flashing a light around and I came over to investigate. Zach's my backup."

"So…" She drew the word out and looked up at Zach. "Nothing's wrong at home?"

"Not a thing."

Zach looked a little too pleased to be throwing Tanner to the wolves…

In this case a very pretty wolf.

"Do you mind telling us what you were doing in this building?" Tanner asked.

She took her time shifting her attention from Zach to Tanner. "Because?"

"This building's been empty a long time. And there's a no-trespassing sign right there." He pointed just beyond Zach as he moved out of the way so she could see the sign.

She saw it, all right. She walked right past them, and despite the cold, harsh wind, she reached up, grabbed the card-stock sign and yanked it down, then tossed it into the wastebasket fastened to the corner post of the building.

"Julia."

Zach rolled his eyes, but he grinned, too, as if he thought her antics were funny. He turned to Tanner and waved as she moved back inside. "Tanner, my sister, Julia. Julia, this is Tanner Reddington. And stop giving him the evil eye. He's one of the good guys."

"He was ready to shoot me," she protested, scowling. "Don't you guys have something better to do than bother a woman when she's trying to measure her new work space?"

New work space?

Tanner looked at her, then the grungy interior. "You're putting a store in here? Really? You must have some serious money you're willing to throw away. If that's your goal—" he raised his hands as if shrugging off the whole affair "—then this is the perfect investment property. I can't think of a worse place for a—"

She didn't let him finish. Instead, she thrust her cell phone into his hand with the flashlight turned on. "A clinic, actually. Here. Hold this.

We'll need light, and with you and Zach here I can get this done and get home."

Bossy and quick, two things he disliked in a woman. "This is nuts. The storm's going to hit any minute."

"I've been called worse." She made Zach hold one end of a measuring tape, then walked the other end to about half the length of the building. "Eighteen feet by thirty-five feet."

"Am I supposed to remember this?" Zach asked.

She brightened immediately. "Perfect, yes! Thank you. And now back here." She moved farther back into the shadows and counted off space, then had Zach help measure while Tanner stood still, the beam aimed in their direction. She nodded, called out two more numbers to Zach and moved back up front. "You guys packing flashlights?"

Tanner withdrew his weapon and turned the flashlight on.

Julia eyed the gun-and-flashlight combo and whistled. "That's some serious flashlight equipment right there."

It was, and the attached light was sometimes a cop's best friend.

She took her phone back and jotted numbers before tucking it away. "That's it."

"For what?"

"If we get snowed in, I can sketch a floor plan over the next two days. Without the numbers, I'd be making assumptions."

"You know there's a storm about to hit us?"

"Hence, my need for speed." Her cool look said her reasoning was obvious and he was crazy.

Her quick dismissal made him want to read her the riot act about safety and good choices, similar to the one he dished out to the junior high health class a few days ago.

"What's with the rental car, Jules?" Zach moved toward the door, aiming his gun-mounted flashlight ahead so they could see their way out.

"My SUV got rear-ended by a drug salesman in a hurry to get home before the weather turned foul. It's going to be in the shop for a week at least."

"Were you in it?" Concern laced Zach's question as Julia turned the key, then tested the door to make sure it locked.

"Nope, it was parked, but he did a number on it."

"You know this sedan drives different on snow and ice," Zach reminded her as they stepped outside. "Don't expect it to respond the same way as your SUV."

"I won't." She turned to face them while the

brisk wind whipped tiny snowflakes through her upswept hair. "I'm heading straight home, and I'll go slow, although now that it's snowing, I'm missing my Forester big-time."

"Just be careful. And who are you getting to do the work here?" Zach asked, and when she answered his question with a pert smile, he scowled. "I was afraid of that. You do know I have a wife and toddler at home, right?"

"Piper offered to help, actually, while Lucia watches Jack. She loves projects like this."

"And what exactly is this project?" Tanner asked as he and Zach made sure her car started all right. "A clinic, you said?"

Her happy answer made him want to turn tail and run, hard and fast.

And not look back.

"A pregnancy center for the poor. We'll service folks who've slipped through the cracks or who've fallen on hard times, or just don't have the means to get things done. We hope to open within a month as long as we can get the setup work done. And while this doesn't look pretty now—" she jutted her chin toward the scruffy strip mall "—we can tackle the outside in the spring. For right now, clean and safe prenatal care is the plan."

Something rose high in Tanner's throat. His heart, maybe?

He'd made it a point to stay away from anything to do with pregnancy and women these past three years. He avoided hospital detail as if it were the plague, he never sat near people with kids—or those expecting babies—anywhere. Ever.

He didn't need reminders of what he'd lost. It was there, every day, in the empty bed he used to share with a beautiful woman. His life, his love, his partner in all things. The extra bedrooms in the sprawling ranch home he'd finally sold over two years ago, his attempt to physically erase brick-and-mortar memories.

Julia gave him an odd look, as if wondering what he was thinking, but then she waved, turned on the engine and headed toward the parking lot exit.

Zach moved to his car. "Hey. It's cold and snowing. Why are you standing there? Let's go grab food at The Pelican's Nest and we can monitor calls from there."

Tanner didn't want food. He didn't want to pretend this was okay.

A pregnancy center, stuck in a boarded-up strip mall, right in the middle of his patrol zone.

He waved Zach off as he climbed into his cruiser. "Not hungry, but thanks. I'll go back to my watch spot near the entrance ramp. That way I'm close if anything goes down at this end of the lake."

Zach gave him a thumbs-up and shut his car door.

Tanner climbed in more slowly.

An hour ago he'd been sitting peacefully, watching conditions worsen, hoping for a quiet night. Now?

He couldn't get Ashley and baby Solomon out of his mind. In less than twenty-four hours, he'd lost his wife and his premature baby boy, tiny and sweet, born too soon.

His heart ached.

He thought he was managing fairly well. Most days he did all right, but the three-year anniversaries were looming.

He moved his cruiser back into position and stared at the low-slung buildings across the two-lane road.

You'll be fine, his conscience assured him. *You've done okay, it's time to move on.*

Tanner hated those words. Lame reassurances from people who hadn't suffered his kind of loss made him want to punch something. He kept a gym membership for that very reason.

Sadness welled within him, but the sorrow had an angry side. A side that railed at God, at medicine, at the timing that changed his life while he'd sat powerless to help.

Ashley gone. Their baby gone. Life alone.

A call on the radio made him pull himself together. A car had gone off the road, just north of the Kirkwood Lake exit. He pulled out of his parking spot, cruised across the lake-spanning highway and headed for the snow-clogged ramp.

Twin headlights stared off to the east, illuminating chunks of ice along the nearby shore.

The car had spun off the bottom of the ramp. Tanner eased around the corner and idled the cruiser, lights flashing. Pulling his hat and gloves on, he hurried across the quickly deepening snow, his flashlight aimed ahead.

The bright beam outlined a silver Chevy that looked familiar. And inside, watching him, was Zach Harrison's sister, Julia.

He tried to wrench her door open. Nothing happened.

She stared up at him, her gaze trusting.

"Can you open the window, Julia?" He shouted the words over the rush of wind.

She shook her head.

He tried to circle the car, but the passenger side was tipped down into the snow, lodged against the embankment. No access there.

He came around front again and called

Zach's phone. Julia's brother answered right away. "Julia's had an accident, she's trapped, she's not in danger, doesn't appear to be badly hurt, but I need her cell phone number. I can't talk to her through the window, the storm's too loud. And then get over here, we're at Exit 8, northbound on Lower Lake Road."

Zach rattled off the number. Tanner heard him hit the siren before he disconnected, and the sound of an approaching ambulance or rescue vehicle told Tanner help was on the way.

He dialed her number and waggled his cell phone for her to see.

She looked startled when her phone rang, groped for it, then shook her head, dismayed. *She can't find the phone.*

He tried again, hoping the ring tone would help her locate the cell. This time she zeroed in on the noise, stretched, and when she sat back up, the look of triumph on her face said she had the phone.

Yes.

He dialed again and she answered quickly. "I'm stuck."

The nonstressed tone of her voice said he wasn't dealing with a typical accident victim, and the look she sent his way, an almost comical look of pleading, said she'd wait for him to rescue her without hysterics.

He liked that.

"Make sure your locks are disengaged from inside."

"I did that. Everything's unlocked. Or should be."

"Try again. Electrical systems can get whacked in an accident."

He saw her hit the button to disengage the locks. She frowned at the door and hit the button again. "It's not responding."

She glared at the console, firmed her chin and stabbed the unlock button with vengeance.

Click.

Tanner caught her smile of success. He spoke into the phone but kept his gaze trained on hers to make sure she understood. "I'm going to climb on top and pull the door. Gravity and the wind will fight me. Are you trapped or can you move to climb out?"

"I can move."

"Okay, when I pull the door, you push it up as hard as you can from inside. Okay?"

"Roger that."

"We don't use radio talk on phones, Julia," he teased, wanting to match her mood. "Every newbie knows that."

"I'm taking it under advisement," she told him. "Umm, I think you should hang up the phone now and rescue me."

"Agreed."

He climbed up the front of the car, moved into position, then reached down and gripped the door handle. He squeezed hard and pulled.

The wind fought him.

The almost upright angle and weight of the door made his task difficult under good conditions. In frigid temps, it was almost impossible.

He wanted her out of the car and in a warm, safe place, fast.

The door moved up.

He clenched tight, bracing himself, because if he lost his grip while Julia climbed out and the door slammed back down, he could seriously hurt her.

He heard a voice, and then he saw gloved fingers, grasping the back side of the driver's door frame. First one hand, then two.

A wind gust buffeted him, jerking him to the left. His foot slipped on a slick spot, but he held tight. *Come on, Julia, grab hold. Climb out. Hang on.*

An arm followed. And then the second arm, grabbing hold of the back door handle, pulling hard.

Her head appeared, then disappeared for long, slow seconds.

That meant something wasn't right. A caught leg, a foot turned wrong.

She disappeared back into the car while Tanner struggled to hold the door open.

The hands appeared again. Then the head, her blond hair whipping in the wind.

This time she made it through the opening, onto the car and slid down into the snow, free.

He let the door down easy, not wanting to rock the car over, then slid down into the snow next to her.

"You're hurt." He stood quickly, hauled her up and pulled her toward his car.

She tried to say something, but the storm stole her words. He tucked her into the front seat of the warm cruiser, circled around and climbed in next to her as the rescue vehicle came into view. He paused, letting heat seep into both of them. "Let me see your face."

"Scratched, banged and bruised, but otherwise unscathed," she assured him, but he reached over, grasped her chin gently and turned her face his way.

He's got gorgeous gray eyes. The kind a girl could get lost in if she had a mind to. Fortunately, I have no such desire.

Hat-matted, snow-flecked hair. Was it dark? Light? She couldn't tell because the dampness made it look dark in the uneven light of the police cruiser.

Square-jawed. Fierce, almost taut features, but as he examined her for damage, the look in his eyes said this warrior had a soft side he hid well.

And that was a relief, because she'd come close to giving him a good, swift kick back in the future pregnancy center.

His broad hands were chilled but gentle. His gaze probed her eyes, and for just a moment she wondered what it would be like to have Trooper Tanner locking eyes with her when he *wasn't* searching for signs of concussion.

"Headache?"

She shook her head, then shrugged. "Well. A little."

"This hurt much?" He touched the side of her face with the pad of his thumb.

"Ouch. Bruised, I expect."

"Oh, yeah. You're gonna have a nice shiner with that one." His smile offered sympathy tinged with sarcasm, a kind of fun mix. "And this?" He sent a light touch over her left eyebrow and seemed happy when she didn't react.

"Should I ask how I look?" She made a face, and he responded with an overdone cringe as if afraid to tell her. She dropped her head back and sighed. "That bad?"

"Two bangs and a bruise. Not too bad. But

wrecking two cars in one day? I'm glad I don't have to pay your insurance, Julia."

"The other one wasn't my fault," she protested. "Parked, I tell you. No way can you pin that one on me."

"And this one?" Tanner slid his gaze to the upended car in front of them.

She sighed out loud. "That one's all me." She started to make a face, but wrinkling the muscles made her temple bruise hurt more so she stopped. "And Zach's going to have a field day because he warned me to handle the car differently."

"Yup."

"Do you have siblings, Tanner?"

"One sister. Neda. She lives in Erie. Just far enough away that she can't remind me of the dumb things I do too often."

As the ambulance crew reached the car, Julia grimaced. "My advice? Keep it that way." She shot a look of chagrin toward Zach's approaching car and winked at Tanner. "Because I'm never going to live this down."

Chapter Two

"I do believe I said no when asked about going to the emergency room." Julia frowned at her watch, then at her brother an hour later. "I have two kids and an overgrown puppy waiting for me at Dad's. And I'm on call for the next forty-eight hours."

"Protocol says head wounds get looked at." Zach aimed one of those brotherly looks her way, the kind that should get him smacked except she was too tired to put up much of a fight. "And you're not on call anymore. I called Dr. Salinas. She's taking calls tonight to give you time to rest."

"You what?" Julia lifted her brows, surprised. "You can't have her do that. She's got a lot on her plate right now. I'm fi—"

"You're not fine," Tanner reminded her. He scanned her face with a mix of sympathy and amusement. "Although I have to hand it to you, you're one tough cookie. And no driving for twenty-four hours. You heard the doctor. How were you expecting to answer calls?"

Great. Just what she needed. Another bossy cop, and he wasn't even related to her.

She was determined to be patient because like it or not, they would be working in the same area, and Julia knew it was way better to have the police on her side. "The doctor didn't mean it."

"I did mean it." The ER doc strode back into the room, handed Julia a container of pain meds, then faced her. "I had them fill this upstairs because the local drugstores are closed due to the storm. Use them if you need them, Julia." His tone and expression said he doubted she would, but should. "I wasn't messing around. No driving for the next twenty-four hours. Go home and rest."

She frowned as she slid off the examining table. Zach held out her coat. She shrugged into it, then turned and stuck her hand out to Tanner. "Thank you for the rescue. I appreciate it. Seeing your lights come across that overpass made me real happy."

The sympathy in his gaze deepened. "Anytime."

"Don't say that," Zach warned. "She's going

to be working under your nose in that new clinic, and Julia's not afraid to lasso people into helping her. Don't make promises you can't keep, Reddington."

"I never do." The promise in his voice pulled Julia's attention up to his eyes. "Call me if you need me, okay?"

Tenderness. Kindness. Warmth. All in a to-die-for package, and when he smiled down at her, the tingle of her palms had nothing to do with a concussion and everything to do with attraction, which couldn't, wouldn't and shouldn't happen. She had a mission to accomplish and despite how broad-shouldered and good-looking Tanner Reddington was, she'd read his dismay back at the clinic. He didn't want her there, and she'd washed her hands of negative men after her ex-husband cheated on her for the second time.

She pulled back, blinked the emotion away and smiled at Zach. "Are you my ride home?"

Zach's radio cued him. He listened, responded and hooked a thumb toward Tanner. "I've got a call across the lake. Tanner, can you get Julia home?"

Tanner saw a shadow of reluctance in Julia's gaze. About riding with him? Going home? He had no idea, but the quick look surprised him. "Glad to. Where's home?"

"I'm on Upper Lake Road, just beyond the Lodge."

Tanner pulled out his hat and gloves, realized Julia had left hers in his cruiser, and handed them to her. "I'll pull my SUV up to the ER entrance so you don't have to walk out in the snow. But wear these until you get to the car because the windchill is wicked."

"But—"

He ignored her protests as he strode into the storm. Five minutes later, he was at the ER door, waiting for her. She climbed in quickly, set his hat and gloves on the space between them, and settled into the seat.

She looked exhausted.

And pretty, despite the banged-up face. The way she sat back, as if allowing herself time to relax didn't happen often, told him Julia Harrison looked after others first, and then maybe took time for herself.

"So, Julia, what do you do, exactly?"

"I'm a midwife and women's health practitioner."

Tanner's fingers tightened around the wheel.

"Our practice was awarded a state grant recently," she went on. "We bought the strip mall location about eight months back. Now we have the approvals in place to get it ready. Once the cleanup work is complete, we'll set up three exam rooms, a waiting room and reception area—"

"With bulletproof glass," he muttered as he made the turn onto Upper Lake Road.

"It's a tough area," she acknowledged, "but I think you run a risk anytime you set up an outreach like this. It didn't stop Mother Teresa, and it didn't stop Jesus." She shrugged. "I like to think this clinic will reflect James's teaching in the Bible. He said faith without works is dead. And while I love our practice, a lot of women don't have the money or insurance to come to our main office, or they shy away because they're afraid they don't fit in. This way, they don't have to do without needed care. And the area isn't as bad as you make out," she added with a pointed look in his direction.

"No?" He wouldn't argue with her because she was fresh out of the hospital, but the lower end of Kirkwood Lake bordered some tough areas of Clearwater. Still, everyone deserved medical care. He believed that. But the thought of a pregnancy center, run by a midwife, right under his nose…

Was this God's idea of a joke? Considering his loss, it felt more like a stab in the back to have Julia Harrison and her health care ideas parked in front of him.

"I think people will be pleased by the idea of medical care at the interstate entrance," she continued. "That way we're only a few minutes' drive for folks in the hills…"

The rural poor of northern Appalachia was a documented fact, a problem that had existed for generations.

"And the people who've fallen on hard times in Clearwater are close, too."

"Plenty of those, unfortunately. The loss of jobs messed up a lot of folks."

"It did." Julia puffed out a breath of air, then turned his way. "But I've always felt that each step we take toward making things better has some good effect. Even if we don't see it."

Was she right?

Tanner wasn't so certain. Was that because of his work, his past? Or was he a negative jerk who always looked at the dark side because he'd been surrounded by that kind of environment as a child? Lately, he wasn't sure. "You're an optimist."

"I hope so." She motioned up ahead. "That's my place on the left, with the red reflectors at the bottom of the driveway." He made the turn up the snow-filled drive, pulled to a stop and she climbed out before he had a chance to get out and open her door.

Her actions said she liked her independence. Five hours ago he might have considered those undesirable qualities in a woman, but seeing how calmly she reacted to the scene at the clinic, then the accident and the hospital—

Maybe a strong, independent woman wasn't a bad thing.

She quirked a grin his way and gave him a quick salute as she grabbed her purse and medical bag, the only things they'd retrieved from her rental car. "Thank you again. I'm sure proximity will mean we see more of each other, and I'm going to hope for two things."

"And they are?"

"First, less snow and ice." She made a face into the driving storm. "And second, if I do run into that trouble you're expecting, you and my brother are around to save me. Again."

Tanner knew that sector as well as anyone. Trouble would find her, no question. Would he be hanging close by to make regular runs to a pregnancy center?

Most likely not, but he didn't need to share that at the moment. "Get inside. Get warm. And good luck finding someone to rent you another car."

She laughed as she dashed up the rest of the driveway and through the garage door.

Lights clicked on inside, behind pulled-back lace curtains.

He considered that as he backed around to pull out of her sloped driveway.

He wouldn't have tagged her as a lace curtain girl. As he drove south toward the interstate, he wondered what else he might have gotten wrong about Julia Harrison.

He pulled into the barracks lot, parked and went inside to complete required paperwork and file his report before he headed home. He didn't want to think about babies and midwives, old dreams and harsh reality. He wanted justice and explanations.

But right now, he wanted a good night's sleep. Restless dreams messed that up. Convoluted images of children and families floated through his brain. Each year he dreaded the double anniversaries. The day he lost his wife, and the day after, when his son took his last breath.

The shift commander called him late morning. "Johnson's out with flu. Can I put you in for an extra afternoon shift today and an overnight tomorrow?"

"Absolutely." He didn't say he'd longed for a call like this. Only the commander in Jamison knew his history, and Alex Steele wasn't the kind to betray a confidence. But Alex could empathize because he knew what it meant to bury a wife. "I'll be there by two."

The work respite pushed him into gear. He'd made it a habit to follow up on accident victims, which meant a quick call to Zach's sister. Mixed emotions rose as he dialed her number on his way to his car. Julia the person was intriguing in multiple ways.

Julia the midwife? Not so much. But that was *his* problem, not hers. She answered on the second ring. "Julia Harrison."

"It's Tanner Reddington, Julia. I wanted to check in and see how you're doing today."

"Before or after the tree fell on my house during last night's storm?"

He stopped walking, certain he'd misunderstood. "What?"

"A tree. Fell on my house."

Was she serious? "Are you okay?"

"Fine. But my house isn't looking all that good right now."

"What happened?" Thoughts of her in danger made his pulse speed up. "Are you sure you're not hurt?"

"No, I'm fine, really. The tree hit one end of the house and I was in the other. But it will be boarded up for weeks while they do repairs, so

I'm staying at my dad's with my two little boys and a somewhat ill-mannered and huge puppy. They're having the time of their lives helping on the farm. The boys, not the dog. He's not exactly mature enough to be farm friendly."

"I'm glad you weren't hurt."

"Even though I'm building a clinic in the middle of the 'hood'?"

"I wouldn't call it the 'hood,' but it's not what we'd call a welcoming neighborhood, either."

"Rehabilitation starts one step at a time," she replied. "And even if we only help save one baby, one woman, it's a job well done."

One baby. One woman.

His belly clenched.

She made it all seem possible, and maybe it was, but then why did he have to face the impossible? His lawyer had emailed him that they needed a conference call to talk about the malpractice suit he'd filed two years before. He'd ignored the message because talking about settlements and money on the anniversaries of his losses made him cringe.

He couldn't utter a rational response. Not around the lump in his throat. He muttered a goodbye to Julia, gathered his things and went to a coffee shop to spend the next ninety minutes alone. With old rock music playing in the background, and folks coming in and out, he could bask in obscurity until he showed up at work. Mercifully, working would help him through the next forty-eight hours.

A call to back up Zach Harrison on a possible breaking and entering case came midway through his shift. He drove toward the lower east side of Kirkwood Lake just after dusk.

He pulled up to the address, spotted Zach's cruiser off to the side and rolled to a stop alongside him. He lowered his window so they could talk without radios. "What have you got?"

"B and E, two kids, a possible third, looting side-by-side merchants."

"You want front or back?"

"I'll take front. Chalmers should be right along."

"They know they've been spotted?"

Zach shook his head. "I'm blocked by the trees. A neighbor in the upstairs apartment over the nail salon called it in. And it's dark now, so they're less likely to see us."

Chalmers pulled up then, and the three men eased out of their SUVs. Tanner circled left while Chalmers joined Zach as they approached the front of the building. Zach stopped, waited for Tanner to make it around back, then yelled, "New York State Troopers! Come out with your hands up!"

They came out, but not with the intention of getting caught. Two darted out the back, straight at Tanner. He raised his hands. "Stop. Now."

One kid did. The other dodged right, then the first one thought that might be a good idea, and darted left. Tanner pinned him against the wall while talking to Zach and Chalmers through his radio. "One suspect heading east, about five-eight, leather jacket, clean-shaven, tight blue jeans, black boots."

Zach's voice came through the radio. "I've got visual."

The next thing Tanner heard was a dash, then a scuffle, followed by a moan of pain. Zach was in trouble. He half dragged his cuffed perp around the front of the building, then groaned.

Zach lay sprawled in hip-deep snow. Chalmers had both youths lying on the ground, his weapon drawn as he barked a request for an ambulance into the radio. And from the look of Zach's lower leg, his ankle went one way and the leg went the other.

Julia Harrison was going to kill Tanner for not protecting her brother. And he wouldn't blame her one bit.

She rushed into the ER twenty minutes later with Zach's wife, Piper, and a big, broad man that must be Zach's father, Marty. He was taller than Julia, with the same blond hair, and he threw a frustrated look at Zach. "First her." He jerked a thumb at Julia. "Now you. I assumed this whole parenthood thing got easier once you grew up. Clearly I was mistaken."

"Are you okay?" Julia asked while Piper grabbed hold of Zach and burst into tears.

Zach sent his father a questioning look because anyone who knew Piper McKinney Harrison knew she didn't cry. Ever.

Marty Harrison made a face, surprised.

Julia shrugged. "Don't look at me. I figured it was just an ankle and not a bullet, but then I'm hard-hearted."

"Compared to Piper?" Tanner scratched the back of his head. "No one's tougher than Piper, are they?"

Julia started to speak, then paused.

Zach winced in pain, then caught her look. "Piper? Are you…? I mean, are we expecting again?"

"Yes." She nodded against his chest, and Tanner's gut did a weird little twist when Zach's hand tightened protectively over his wife's neck. "I was going to tell you tonight,

I had it all planned and it was going to be very romantic—"

"Seems it already was," noted Julia. Her easy humor made Tanner feel better, but for a guy who avoided pregnancy and children purposely, he'd been unexpectedly bombarded by both for the past twenty-four hours.

"And then they called and said you were hurt," Piper continued, "and the first thing I thought was you were shot."

"But I wasn't."

"Well, you *could* have been," she insisted.

"Only if Tanner shot me. Or Chalmers. Unfortunately I was bested by a decorative rock path buried under a monumental snowdrift. I went one way. My foot went the other."

"How bad is it?" Julia asked. She lifted the blanket, grimaced and set the woven throw back down gingerly. "Oh, that'll need an operation, bro. When is that expected to happen?"

A doctor strode into the room. "Right now. We just called in an ortho specialist. I'm Dr. Laramie, hey, wait." He stared at Tanner, then Julia, then Zach. "Didn't I see you Three Musketeers in here last night?"

"Guilty as charged," Tanner admitted. "Last night it was her fault." He pointed Julia's way and ignored her little squawk of protest. "This one's on me."

"It's on a rock path and a snowstorm and three brats who wanted to steal old folks' pensions to support a drug habit." Zach held Piper's hand between two of his and stared at Tanner. "You had two-on-one at the back. You did what you needed to do. I tripped, plain and simple."

Tanner couldn't let it go that easily. "If he'd come around the other way, you'd have been clear and there'd be no injury. Now you're busted, your wife's expecting and you won't be around to back me up for six—"

"Eight," said Zach's father.

Julia scoffed. "Ten, minimal."

"Twelve weeks, most likely," the doctor advised cheerfully. He held up an X-ray. "This snazzy black-and-white photo of your bones shows multiple breaks that are going to be surgically repaired by installing some pretty inventive hardware in your ankle. The nuts and bolts will hold things together as they heal, but the tough part isn't the four breaks in the bone."

"It's not?" Zach asked.

"Soft tissue damage," the doctor reported. "That's why we're looking at twice the healing time. Tendons and ligaments grow slowly, so you'll be spending the entire spring out of commission."

Zach looked like someone just kicked him in the teeth, and Tanner knew just how he felt. Twelve weeks of immobility?

A killer.

Zach turned toward his sister. "Julia. The clinic." His face darkened. "Oh, man. You were counting on me, and you need to have that work done on time for the grant money to be disbursed."

She waved his concern off as if it was nothing, and that garnered Tanner's respect because Zach had explained that if the work didn't get done, the grant money went to someone else.

"You think you're indispensable or something?" Julia shrugged as if this wasn't a big deal, but Tanner knew better. "We'll get someone else to help us get the clinic ready for business."

"I know what your budget's like and you were counting on me," Zach lamented. "And we can't have Piper working in a zone that might have asbestos. Jules, really, I'm so sorry."

"I'll help" Tanner offered. It was the last thing he wanted to do, to be caught in a work zone with midwives and doctors and pregnant women, but they should be done with the work before too many young mothers came around. "I'm decent with a hammer and I like fixing things. And it's not bragging to say I'm better than your brother."

Zach started to protest, but Tanner stopped him. "Save your breath. If I'd been between the kids and that alley, the second kid wouldn't have gone that way and you'd be doing paperwork right now. As it is, Chalmers is doing paperwork and I'm…" He took a deep breath. "Going to help build walls for a women's health clinic in a crime-riddled strip mall."

"Not necessary," Julia said coolly. "But thank you. I'm sure I'll have plenty of help, and didn't we confirm last night that accidents happen to everyone? No one's fault, then or now." Her expression said she didn't need his help or like his attitude. But he knew what he needed to do.

"I will help, it's useless to argue," Tanner offered mildly. "And who's got your boys and little Jackson if you're all here?"

"My mother." Piper kissed Zach's cheek as the doctor returned with papers to sign. "She's having the time of her life, and she can't wait to be a grandma again."

Tanner had had enough talk of babies and clinics. He'd been so happy to get the call-in today, glad to push thoughts of this anniversary aside, but that was hard when pregnancy chatter surrounded him. He took a step backward.

"Zach, I'm heading out to help Chalmers. I'll do whatever you need, and again, I'm sorry, man."

Zach waved him off. Tanner started to head toward Julia, but her expression said their conversation was over.

It wasn't over, it had barely begun, and he had every intention of helping with her women's health center. Why it had to be in his patrol area was a quirk of fate he didn't need, but out of his control.

He strode out the door, determined. Like it or not, Zach had gotten hurt because he'd messed up. Now he'd help pick up the slack his mistake had caused. Whether Julia liked it or not.

Chapter Three

Julia stopped by her house on the way home from the hospital. The emergency enclosure firm had battened down the hatches and the firefighters had removed the tree and secured the electric lines, but it would be weeks before her house was habitable. She hurried upstairs, grabbed clothing and toiletries she'd need for herself and the boys, then saw the message light flashing on her landline as she descended the stairs.

She hit the message code. The unexpected tones of her ex-husband's voice made her chest ache. "Ignoring me, Julia? Doing what you do best, hiding your head in the sand to avoid reality? Well here's the deal, Martin and Connor are my kids as much as yours, and if I have to go to a judge to enforce my visitation rights, I'll do it. Don't make me bring you to court, Julia. Call me and set up a time for me to have my sons. We'll meet somewhere in the middle."

Julia's heart froze solid, the phone in her hand.

Meet in the middle?

Did Vic expect her to drive halfway to Ithaca and hand Martin and Connor over to him after he'd spent the past two years ignoring them?

Not gonna happen.

Ice pulsed through her veins as she smacked down the phone. The sound of his voice was antagonistic, and condescending, as if distancing herself from his affairs was an over-reaction on her part.

She paced the long living room, examining her options.

Vic had visitation rights, but he'd never bothered to use them. He'd shrugged off her moving to Kirkwood Lake two years ago, and other than the infrequent child support checks, he'd stayed out of their lives.

Until now.

Why now?

She didn't have a clue. Her head hurt but she wasn't about to take one of those pain pills and cloud her thinking.

The phone rang.

She jumped, stared at the caller ID and

heaved a sigh of relief when her father's number flashed. "Hey, Dad."

"Hey yourself. You okay? I thought you just had to grab a few things. Need me to come around that way?"

"No, but thanks. I'm fine."

"You don't sound fine, Jules." Her father wasn't the kind of guy anyone fooled for long. "You sound like you're ready to pop someone in the jaw."

Her father knew her well.

"Is your head hurting? Do you need me to drive you back here?"

"No, nothing like that." She paused, then blew out a breath. "Vic called."

Marty Harrison growled. "He hasn't contacted you in over a year."

"Almost eighteen months, and that was to explain why he couldn't take the boys for their two-week summer visit because he was too busy finishing up his course work to become a school administrator."

"I remember. What does he want?"

"He wants the boys over spring break. And he says he wants his one weekend a month like the court promised."

"Now? After all this time? Why?"

Julia had no answers. Only more questions. "I don't know."

Her father breathed deeply, then offered typical Marty Harrison wisdom. "Well, we know he wants something. Vic is nothing if not predictable, but there's no sense worrying about it tonight. You need to sleep and we'll tackle this tomorrow. Let him stew on it overnight, Jules."

"Which means we both stew on it."

"Trials of parenthood, honey. No one said it would be easy."

True, but then no one warned her that her good-looking, high school teacher husband would stray outside their marriage. Call her naive, but being raised in the Harrison house, good men didn't do things like that. Which meant she'd either placed her trust foolishly...

Put a check in the yes column on that one!

Or she wasn't as slim or attractive as she'd been when they dated nine years before.

Another check in the yes column, with a helping of self-recrimination poured on top, like chocolate glaze on a doughnut.

"And stop beating yourself up, Julia. That's not how I raised you."

"My spunk's on low tonight, Dad. It's been a rough forty-eight hours."

"You escaped two car wrecks and a falling tree with nothing more than a couple of cuts, bruises and bangs. Pretty positive result in my book, kid."

She laughed because he was absolutely right. "Two of which were not my fault, of course."

"And neither was the broken marriage," Marty told her bluntly. "We'll figure this out in the morning. I love you, honey."

"Love you back. I'll be at your place in a few minutes."

She hung up and stared at boarded up wall in front of her.

Broken and battered. Her heart had felt like that wall when she'd realized Vic had cheated for the second time.

Was she unlovable? Not pretty enough? Not thin enough? Gone too much? What did these other women have that she didn't?

Why does it have to be about you? Why can't it be about him? Maybe some guys are just jerks?

Rational argument said Vic Gentry *was* a two-timing jerk. But in the cold light of day, her heart knew what her head denied: he hadn't just turned *to* others.

He'd turned *away* from her. And she wasn't at all sure she wasn't somewhat to blame for that.

"Oh. 'Scuse me!"

A miniature version of Julia's blue eyes under a mop of blond curls met Tanner's eyes as they collided at Zach's side door the next afternoon. "Whoa. I gotcha, bud."

"Connor? Are you okay?" Julia's voice called from somewhere inside Zach's house.

The little boy rolled his eyes. "I'm fine! I'm going to see if Beansy's friend had her babies yet."

"Go across lots, not around the road."

"Mom, I know all this stuff. I'm five! I'm not a baby."

"Didn't say you were, and—" Julia stopped as she got to the side door, looking surprised to see him. "Tanner. I'm sorry, I didn't know you were here."

"Julia." He nodded toward the kid. "Yours?"

"On good days." She grinned at the boy and laid her hand on top of his head. "Be good for Grandpa, okay?"

"Grandpa and me work together on weekends." He pulled a knit hat down on his head and stood as tall and straight as a kid could while he addressed Tanner. "He's teaching me everything about farming."

"I expect he's mighty pleased to have a helper like you around," Tanner said.

"Two helpers." Connor shoved his feet into old-fashioned rubber farm boots. "Martin's already over there, checking on the mommy goat, but I had to practice my reading words.

Which was kinda dumb because I knew them all already." He darted a dark glance at his mother, a look she ignored completely. He raced out the door, then stopped and stuck out a little hand in Tanner's direction.

"I'm Connor."

"My name's Tanner. Nice to meet you."

"Do you like goats?"

"More than life itself," Tanner replied with a quick side smile toward Julia.

Connor leaned in as if sharing a very big secret. "We're going to have baby goats soon. And baby goats are called kids just like kids are called kids."

Tanner offered the boy an exaggerated look of surprise, as if Connor's revelation was truly amazing.

"And they're going to get born, like, any day now. Maybe even today." He gave Julia a miffed look. "My mom delivers babies but she says Daisy is better having her babies on her own because goats know how to do those kind of things. Do you think they do?"

He shrugged. "It makes sense, I guess."

"Well, I hope so because I've been waiting for these babies a very long time." Connor's serious expression mirrored his words. "Every day I pray and pray for these babies, and she hasn't had them yet."

"Animals have been giving birth forever." Julia's calm tone said nature would prevail. "I expect Miss Daisy will be fine, Connor. And if there's an emergency, I can be on call, okay?"

"Except she's all alone at night," the boy muttered as he pushed out the door. "So I don't know who's going to take care of her then and I know Grandpa'd let us bring her in the basement. Just until."

"God will take care of her," Julia suggested as if God could be counted on for everything.

Tanner knew better.

The boy's scowl said he sided with Tanner. The door banged shut behind him as Julia stepped aside. "The patient awaits. Zach was excited that you were coming over."

"You're on nursing duty today?"

"Well, he's out of my area of expertise, but I figured whining's whining and he's not all that different than the five-year-old that just scolded me on his way out the door."

"I'm not whining." Zach made a face as they walked into the living room. "I'm too drugged up to whine properly. Give it a week."

"I can hardly wait." Julia stage-whispered the words. "I can disappear and give you guys time to visit if you've got sensitive cop stuff you need to discuss."

"We don't, but thanks. Tanner, you want

coffee? Tea? Piper made a pitcher of tea this morning because the long winter is getting on her nerves."

"I'm sure it has nothing to do with the grumbling husband stuck in the living room." Julia grinned at him from across the room and added, "I kind of love that you're trapped. How mean is that? I can sling sisterly barbs in your direction and you're pretty much helpless."

Zach glowered at her, but Tanner saw the sparkle in his eyes as well, a look that said he loved his sister.

Tanner loved his sister, too. He and Neda did everything together as kids, and he'd even walked her down the aisle at her wedding. But now he shied away from her because she had two little ones. He was missing a lot of life in his self-imposed cocoon.

"Tanner. You told me you have a sister, right?" Zach asked.

"I did say that."

"Is she a pain in the neck?"

"Definitely."

"Does she bake you brownies with walnuts and chocolate chips?" Julia brought a plate over and set it on the small table they'd rigged next to Zach's recliner. "And bring you the latest Sudoku puzzles to keep your mind sharp while you while away the next few months?

And did she or did she not give you a gift subscription to Netflix?"

"Once I'm awake enough to watch anything, I'll thank you." Zach gave her a tired smile. "You know I'm grateful. Just a little grumpy and medicated."

"Blah, blah, blah." She leaned over and kissed Zach's forehead, winked at Tanner and started to leave, but Zach called her back.

"Julia, sit a minute. I want to hear your plans for the clinic, and with Tanner helping—"

"Not necessary, but again, thank you for offering." She shot a bright smile at Tanner, but he wasn't about to be sloughed off. Helping out was something he wanted and needed to do, for his own peace of mind.

"I'm good for grunt work." He said it mildly but made sure she knew he wasn't about to budge. "So what's the configuration you took to the town for approval?"

She looked trapped.

Good.

He might hate the idea of having a pregnancy center there. But he wasn't against health care, so he'd swallow his personal misgivings and man up.

"A small reception area with about a dozen seats around the perimeter. Then a short hall with an exam room on either side, and one at the base of the hall."

"T-shaped formation."

"Yes. And an alcove for weigh-ins, drawing blood, entering notes into the system."

"System?"

She nodded. "The grant covers a computer system that's integrated with the main computer at the home office. We'll be able to enter data from both sites."

"Will the computers be locked up at night?" She frowned.

"To thwart things like what happened four blocks away when Zach got hurt." He indicated Zach with a glance. "Visible equipment makes you an easier target for thieves."

"They'll be built in, actually."

"Hardwired?" Zach asked.

She stared at him blankly. "What does that mean?"

Zach laughed without thinking, then grimaced in pain. "That means built right into the electrical system. No plugs."

"Yes. I'm sorry, I thought you realized, but we upgraded right after Jack was born so you haven't seen the new computers. And these machines wouldn't do anyone any good, actually." She brought her attention back to Tanner. "They're not meant for anything other than entering and transferring patient records, so why would anyone want to steal them?"

"First, you're giving thieves way more credit for brains than most of them deserve," Tanner told her. "And second, on the black market, everything has a price and a buyer, if for nothing else than to hold information hostage."

"Why would anyone do that?"

Zach and Tanner spoke in unison. "Money."

She pressed her lips together as reality hit home. "I guess that's a risk we have to take."

"Not if you go old-school and use paper at the clinic, then have someone update at the main office each day."

"Who has time for that?" Julia directed the question to Zach but stared at Tanner.

"That's what a lot of practices did until a few years ago," he reminded. "I'm not telling you how to do your job, Julia, but I'm looking at this from a police perspective. Out of sight is always better. Lessen the temptation, you avoid the crime."

"So we have to either hire a data input person to transfer files at the main office each day or risk a B and E"?

"If you have part-time personnel, couldn't they tack an extra five hours onto their weekly schedule to upload daily information?"

Now she looked interested. "You know, that

might work, Tanner. We have a couple of people who might benefit from those five extra hours. And if we didn't have to expand the integrated system, we could use the money for something else."

"Everyone's happy that way." Tanner reached for a brownie. "Would you care to join me in a celebratory brownie?"

She eyed the plate, then shook her head. "I'm going to pass." She stood, glanced at her watch and said, "Actually, Zach, I'm going to head to the gym as long as Tanner's here and the boys are with Dad. Call my cell if you need anything. Tanner, are you okay here for half an hour, give or take?"

He hoisted the tray of brownies. "Preseason baseball on cable and these. We're good."

She grabbed her purse, gave the brownies one last look and started for the door.

"When do we start demolition?"

"Soon, but I have to check Dad's schedule."

He made a "call me" sign with his right hand. The move made her laugh, but it wasn't hard to see the shadows in her eyes. She left and he turned to Zach. "Does she hate me?"

"Julia doesn't hate anyone, not even her stupid ex-husband who cheated on her, made her feel like dirt, and ignored his kids for over two years and now expects her to jump through hoops so he can visit them."

Tanner held up a hand. "I'm going to stop asking you questions because the meds have unhinged your tongue and your sister might kill you for telling me all that."

"All what?"

Zach looked confused, which meant the meds were doing a number on him. Tanner grabbed the remote, turned on a preseason Pittsburgh game and settled into the wide-armed chair with the tray of brownies close. "Baseball it is, my friend."

But Zach's words ignited a curl of sympathy wrapped around a thread of anger. What kind of idiot cheated on a beautiful woman like Julia and ignored his kids? The thought of a father dismissing his children frustrated him. He'd never had the chance to carry, rock or play with baby Solomon.

A tiny part of him wondered, for just a moment, if maybe Sol and Ashley were together in heaven. If maybe, just maybe, she was holding their son in her arms, and whispering stories about his dad on Earth.

He shoved the sentimental thoughts away, but as he did, a cardinal lit on the tree outside Zach's front window. The red bird danced, waved a wing, then danced on the branch again.

Beauty in everyday things.

Ashley had talked about that all the time, and he thought she was being cute and fanciful, but right now, seeing the bird, imagining Sol tucked in Ashley's arms made it almost seem possible.

The game came on and when he glanced back up, the cardinal was gone.

For a moment he'd felt hopeful, as if there might be more to this life than he believed.

But that was probably nonsense, whereas baseball was real, so he concentrated on team rivalries because he understood that.

Life and faith, intertwined? Not so much.

Sixty minutes of exercise did nothing but make Julia hungrier.

She'd ignored the brownies.

She'd turned away from the fresh hoagie bread her father brought home from the McKinney Dairy Farm store, baked daily by an Amish woman over on County Road 4.

She'd grabbed a pack of fresh veggies, told herself that cucumbers were the new chocolate, but it was no use. She needed coffee, *good* coffee, and she needed it now. The best place to find that was at Tina's Corner Café. The popular gathering spot was now tucked into an expanded corner of The Pelican's Nest, a family owned restaurant on the shores of Kirkwood Lake. No way was she going back home without a proper caffeine fix and maybe some girl talk. Knowing she was going to be working side by side with a grumpy cop and trying to analyze Vic's moves made the company of other women essential.

She walked through the door, smiled at Tina, looked at Tina's aunt Laura and promptly burst into tears.

"Julia! Sweetie, what is it?" Laura wrapped her arms around Julia and hugged her close. "Are you okay? Are the boys okay? Is it Zach? Or your father?"

Julia shook her head, tried to talk, failed miserably, then sighed when Tina handed over a fistful of tissues. "Men." Tina muttered the word with typical Martinelli emphasis. "Can't live with 'em. Can't shoot 'em."

"Which of course would be a dreadful sin," added Laura, "but if some wretched man has broken your heart, honey, I'm not afraid to help make his life miserable, and I'll do it in the most sincere manner a Sunday-school teaching woman can employ and stay right with God."

Julia burst out laughing. The thought of sweet, mild-mannered Laura D'Allesandro taking up Julia's cause sounded real good right now. "I'll be fine, and yes, it's a man. How did you know?" she asked, and Tina just rolled her eyes.

"Let's just say I used to be familiar with the symptoms. Before Max, that is." She smiled when she mentioned her husband's name. "I've kissed a few frogs in my time."

"Kiss a few toads, sweep our share of ashes," Laura exclaimed with a quick swipe of a washcloth to the empty tables.

"But you didn't marry the frogs," Julia reminded Tina. "You waited for the prince to come along."

Tina's expression said otherwise. "I was engaged to one and almost engaged to the other. So pretty close, darling."

"You're among friends, now tell us. What's going on?" Laura asked. "You're never upset, you're the most even-keeled, optimistic person I know. This has got to be really nasty to have you this riled up."

"Coffee, first," Tina inserted. "I think a caramel macchiato would be just right."

Julia glanced up at the calorie board and hesitated.

Tina groaned.

Laura sighed. "Don't tell me a pretty thing like you is worried about her weight? Because I'll just fall down laughing."

"And I'll join her, and then there'll be no

one to make your coffee," Tina continued. She reached out and grabbed Julia's hands as Julia sank onto a counter stool. "I don't know the story, but I'm going to guess he cheated on you and you're trying to figure out why."

Julia stared at her. "How did you know that?"

"Because women tend to assume it's our fault first." Tina moved back behind the counter and started building Julia's drink. "We see their cheating as the result of our lack, instead of their choice to stray."

"Which is ridiculous, of course," Laura chimed in. "What does God tell us about women in Proverbs 31? That a woman opens her hands to the poor and reaches out to the needy. That she works for her family, and provides for them? I don't recall seeing anything about being a size six, Julia. Or trying to reform ourselves to win affection. Shouldn't we be loved as God loves us? For ourselves?"

"It's wonderful in theory." Julia smiled at Tina when she set the steaming caramel coffee in front of her. "Unfortunately reality says something different these days."

"My dose of today's reality is to head to work."

The sound of Tanner's voice made all three

ladies turn as he came around the corner from the main restaurant dining area.

Laura smiled. Clearly familiar with Tanner's tastes, Tina called a greeting, grabbed a large to-go coffee cup and moved to the espresso machine.

Julia was glad she hadn't been griping about Tanner when he walked in. She met his eyes as he approached the coffee counter. "Thanks for hanging with Zach this afternoon."

"Piper's stepmother came over to make sure he was doing okay. He drifted in and out of sleep the whole time I was there, which meant I could cheer for the Pirates and no one reamed me out. I found it oddly disappointing."

"You'll be safe for a while because he'll be on heavy-duty pain meds for days." Julia sipped her coffee, glad she hadn't insisted on the plain black version. This amazing concoction was so much better. Or maybe it was her proximity to this puzzling man with soft but tough gray eyes. "But he'll be glad you came by, Tanner."

Tina extended his coffee across the curved wooden coffee bar and waved off his money. "You know better, even though you're not at this end of the lake all that often," she teased. "Coffee for cops is on the house."

"You just want me to be nice to Max, since he's new on the force."

"After ten years of military special ops, I can assure you that Max Campbell has plenty of tricks up his sleeve," Tina told him, "so I'd be careful treating him like a normal probie. Just a word to the wise."

"I got to work with him last month." Tanner raised his coffee cup in salute. "And he did okay. For a military guy."

Tina laughed. "I won't tell him you said so because I know how the loyalty game plays out. But just so you know, he spoke well of you, too."

Tanner grinned. He turned back toward Julia. "According to your father, I'll see you Tuesday night. Six o'clock. Your place."

He aimed a smile at the two women behind Julia, then walked out. Julia read their expressions, and put up her hands. "It's not what you think, even though he's funny, gentle, sensitive and wretchedly good-looking."

"It should be." Laura exchanged a look with Tina, a look that said Tanner Reddington was positively swoon-worthy. "Oh, honey, I promise you. It should be."

"I have enough on my plate right now." Julia watched Tanner as he crossed the parking lot. Tall, square-shouldered and decisive, he looked as good from behind as he did from the front, but something in his reticence tripped mental red flags. She switched her attention back to the women. "For the moment I'm trying to figure out what my ex-husband is up to all of a sudden. There is no time in the world for that. Unfortunately." She waved toward the door Tanner had just closed.

"Mmm-hmm." Laura's knowing smile said she wasn't buying it. Tina's said the same.

For a moment, Julia wondered if that gleam in Tanner's eye went deeper than gentle amusement. Was he interested in her?

Of course not. He was always one step shy of rude during their conversations, and what she absolutely, positively did not want, ever again, was to have to prove herself to a man, because Laura was right. God's command to man was to cherish women, to love them as he loved the church.

She'd lived that failure once. She never wanted to face that outcome again.

Chapter Four

Tanner steered his car off of Main Street and onto Lower Lake Road.

Two years of silence.

Zach's careless remark had been on his mind for over an hour. A beautiful woman, smart and funny, unafraid to joke around. Two kids. What kind of man walked away from that? Or ignored his kids?

It wasn't his business. But the idea of someone ignoring their kids made him want to pummel something. For three long years he'd asked himself what he could have done differently.

Insisting that Ashley see a regular obstetrician instead of a midwife might have been a good start.

He knew that. He'd had misgivings from the beginning. He'd wanted a full-fledged doctor, the best available. Wouldn't that have been the most sensible option? But Ashley had been so sure in her choices, so caught up in the research of natural methods. Would a different medical professional have seen signs of trouble before it had gone too far?

He didn't know, but old regrets speared deep.

His cell phone interrupted his thoughts.

"Tanner, it's Captain Steele. How're you doing?"

Had the Troop A boss remembered the anniversary of his wife's death, with all he had to do and oversee? Appreciation eased the weight on his chest. "Okay. Counting the hours. Breathing."

Alex Steele's voice deepened. "I know. I remember. You working today?"

"Got called in. Yesterday and today, so that's better than sitting home. Pretending to be busy."

"I intend to keep you busier," Alex said. "We're forming a collaborative task force to address the burglaries and increased drug use in your sector of Clearwater. You're familiar with the neighborhoods and the people. We'll be working with the Clearwater police and the sheriff's office. You want in?"

"Absolutely, especially if it helps us get a lockdown on juvenile crime. It's been an epidemic lately."

"I want to jump on this so we have a head start before the weather gets nice," Alex told him. "I'll be in touch."

"Thanks, Captain."

"No thanks needed. A great record and clean arrests earned you the spot. And, Reddington?"

"Yes?"

"You're on my prayer list. Hang in there."

Tanner had no clue what to say to that, but the captain hung up before he needed to respond.

Prayer list?

Yeah, right. Good luck with that. He drove past several nice-looking churches, purposely ignored them, and headed for the southern tip of the lake.

He and his sister, Neda, had been used as pawns between his parents for years. No matter how much he prayed as a kid, nothing got better in the back-and-forth of court dates, custody battles and child support hearings.

He'd learned to stand on his own two feet and avoid drama. And if he'd ever wondered about the essence of God, the humility of faith as an adult?

It all went by the wayside when Ashley and little Solomon breathed their last breaths. Lingering thoughts and doubts vanished. He'd face the world alone, like he'd been doing for a very long time. He was okay with that.

Julia saw Tanner's name in her phone display that evening. Her pulse jumped, because why would he be calling her now? Maybe the gals at the café were right. Maybe— "Tanner. Hi. What's up?"

His reply pretty much dashed Laura's and Tina's notions like waves on the eastern shore. "I've got a Tuesday night work conflict that just came up, so I was wondering if we could do teardown on Wednesday evening instead?"

A work conflict that came up on Sunday? What were the odds of that? So much for thinking she saw a glimmer of interest back at the café. "No worries. Dad and I will charge in on Tuesday as planned and you take care of things at work."

He sighed, a king-size one tinged with amusement, and she almost found herself smiling. "I'm *not* ditching you. We've got a new task force forming and the initial meeting has been scheduled for Tuesday night, so if you know anything about my commander or my job, when they say jump? I jump. So could we possibly move the demolition of the current interior walls to Wednesday night? Because I intend to be there."

"I'm on call Wednesday evening, one of the doctors is manning the Wednesday night crew, so we can't. And like I said, we should be fine, Tanner. There's no reason for you to feel guilty. We've got this."

Silent moments stretched between them. She could picture those deep gray eyes reading between the lines, quietly assessing the situation. "Then I'll catch the next round of work," he said.

"Perfect." Arguing with him would be rude, and they could use his help. Being stubborn about his initial reaction wasn't in the clinic's best interests. And the fact that he was being nicer about the whole endeavor was a plus. Yes, she'd let her imagination get the better of her, thinking he was calling for more personal reasons. Her problem, not his.

"Dad and Luke Campbell will be there Thursday morning. I've got an early appointment, but then I'll be there later in the day."

"Luke, the deputy sheriff?"

"Yes."

"I'll join their crew, then."

"All right." She hung up just as Martin and Connor burst through the side door.

"No babies yet!" Connor announced as he kicked one boot left and the other boot right. "Grandpa looked at her and said it might be a while before they come, but that Rosalita was going to have her calf tonight and if it wasn't too late, I could go out to the barn and see it."

"Because we can't be up late with school tomorrow." Martin hung his coat up, put his boots by the fire and grabbed a cookie. "I want to make sure I get to bed on time so I don't feel tired in the morning."

Her boys were polar opposites. Connor exploded onto every scene, ready to jump in, ignoring danger, laughing in the face of adversity.

Seven-year-old Martin quietly surveyed life from a distance, assessed everything around him, and then made a well-thought-out decision with as little risk as he could find. Some days they got along. Others? Not so much.

"Connor, put your boots where they belong, please."

He rolled his eyes, waited until she asked him a second time, then made an elaborate show of stowing the boots, a task that could have been completed in under ten seconds if he'd avoided the drama. Connor thrived on drama, as long as he was the one causing it.

Martin picked up his e-reader, curled up in the corner of Grandpa's reclining love seat and started to read.

Connor raced to the lower level, pulled out

train tracks and construction worker toys, and built the noisiest city he could fit between Marty's furniture.

Martin went on reading, oblivious.

They were like night and day, but Martin had been especially sensitive to his father's abandonment. Was that his nature or simply because he was older and more aware? How would they handle this new development? How could she make it better for them?

First, she had to talk to Vic calmly and rationally. Then she'd throw something.

With God, all things are possible.

She knew that. Believed it. But she'd witnessed medical emergencies that defied the odds and went bad. She'd seen behavior unbecoming of God's people. She'd treated victims of violence with no explanation of why humans could do such things to one another.

She believed in God, and she was determined to pull her strength from him, but the actions of men were more questionable. Her job was to help her boys grow up as best she could. And pray. But first she'd have to call Vic to see what they could work out.

Once the boys were asleep, she took the phone upstairs. Her hope that he wouldn't answer and she could leave a message was dashed at his quick hello.

"Vic, it's Julia."

"Well, it's about time. You got a new number."

She wasn't about to launch into an explanation of why she was calling from her father's phone. "The old one still works but we had some storm damage so I'm using this one for now."

"Did you get my letter?"

The question surprised her. "No."

"Tomorrow, then. My attorney advised me to send a registered letter to show my intent, which means if you don't show up with the boys, you're in contempt of the visitation agreement. It seemed prudent when I didn't hear from you."

Impatient. Cryptic to the point of rude. Old feelings rushed back. He'd always wanted the upper hand. It was his way or the highway. Why hadn't she seen that sooner?

"Don't you think it would be better to reintroduce yourself to the boys a little at a time?" she suggested. "Call them. Do a face-to-face computer chat with them. Talk to them. Martin remembers you but Connor only knows you from your picture on their wall. I think that would be better for them, Vic. Don't you?"

He let her know in harsh words that he had court-appointed rights. "And furthermore," he reamed her, "I'm not the one that moved three hours away. That was all you, Julia, so just the idea that I'm required to meet you halfway ticks me off. I shouldn't have to step foot out my door, but now I'll spend an entire evening driving across the state and back. So don't talk to me about easy. You gave that all up when you moved so far away."

"Just looking to manage crowd control," she answered smoothly. "I didn't need our boys running into any of your ex-girlfriends when half the town knew what was going on. Making their life less awkward was the goal."

"Babying them is more like it, which is exactly your style. It's a good thing I made sure we stopped at two because I guarantee that's all you could handle."

His words fired a direct shot on her heart. She'd lost their first baby, a tiny girl, miscarried midway through the pregnancy. The devastating loss left a hollow ache in its wake, wondering what her daughter would have been like. Would she like dancing or prefer soccer? Would she sing off-key like Grandpa or join the choir? She would never know these things about her, gone so quickly. Never cuddled, never rocked, never nurtured at her mother's breast.

And then Vic announced after Connor's

birth that he'd gone through surgery to prevent more children without consulting her. He'd decided two kids were plenty, and her dreams of having a little girl someday disappeared. She choked back a heated response, knowing he wanted to make her angry, but refusing him that satisfaction. "This call isn't about my parenting. It's about compromise."

"Well, compromise this, Julia." Then Vic hung up on her.

She stared at the phone, drew a breath and sat on the edge of the bed in the spare room. The short conversation hit multiple emotional buttons, exactly how Vic wanted it to go.

But you don't have to give him that control anymore. Look forward. Seize the days. Pray for him. And break something quietly if you must.

That thought made Tuesday night's demolition much more attractive.

Chapter Five

Surprise and welcome marked Julia's face when Tanner walked into the construction site on Tuesday evening. "You're here."

Her sweet expression made pushing command for an earlier meeting time worth the questioning looks Tanner got from his boss. "I explained what I was doing tonight, how it would benefit the community, and the captain moved the meeting up an hour. So I'm here."

She looked amazed that he would plead his case to his bosses, and that made him wonder how often Julia Harrison had taken a backseat to others. Too often, from what he'd gleaned so far. "Where's your dad?"

"Problem with a cow. If all goes well he should be here later."

"He let you come here alone?" Protective hackles rose along the back of Tanner's neck because that wasn't just dumb, it was dangerous.

"It is quite possible that my father thought you were still coming." She made a face like a kid caught in a cookie jar, then offered her explanation. "It's this deadline thing for the grant. We have to be at certain points by scheduled dates or there is no grant money, so I can't afford to let things get off track."

"This is *not* a safe area," Tanner countered. "And that is magnified by a woman being here alone. At night. Are you always this stubborn?"

"Unfortunately, yes. It's a family trait, I'm afraid."

He recognized the truth in that, but a big burly weapon-carrying cop like Zach stood a much better chance at self-defense than a pretty blonde woman with great eyes. "Promise me you won't do this again. I get that I hurt your feelings by thinking this wasn't the best location for your clinic—"

"Which wasn't your business."

"True. But we need to call a truce if we're going to work together. You need to trust me." The hesitancy in her eyes said that wasn't as easy as he'd hoped it would be. "And I need to trust your goals to help women when they need it."

She met his gaze. "That's a funny way of putting it."

"Not from my point of view. So here. Tonight." He picked up a dust mask and handed her one. "Point me to the right wall. I'm in the right frame of mind to break things and pretty eager to get started."

Julia handed him one of the bigger sledgehammers once they had the masks and gloves on, and made a fierce face. "Me, too."

The face made him laugh. "We have more in common than we might have thought. I like that."

"Ditto." She looked up at him, over the mask, eyes bright. For long, noisy ticks of the old wall clock he stood, looking down, watching her, wondering when his heart had started beating again, but glad it did. "Ready?" She tipped her head toward the wall.

Ready for the feelings she evoked? Ready for a chance to move forward? He wasn't quite sure.

He moved to the wall, raised the hammer and let the blunt force of heavy metal strike the wallboard. It cracked instantly, spewing a cloud of dust into the air. "I'm ready."

She laughed, moved to her wall and mimicked his stance. It took her more than one blow to create a similar-sized hole, but when she did, she aimed a look of triumph his way. "I think we've got this."

And smiling at her, he couldn't disagree.

"Are you still there?" Julia peered through the dust-filled air an hour later.

"I'm here. Six feet to go. And if you're getting tired, put the hammer down."

"And pick up a shovel," she noted. "I'm tired, my upper body is clearly not meant for hours of sledgehammer work, but I can't wait to see the new walls in place! I'll load the wheelbarrow for a bit."

"That's not resting."

"A change is as good as a rest."

Tanner moved closer, grasped her dusty shoulders and looked down. The skip of her pulse said she liked making eye contact with Tanner, even through dust-filled air without her glasses on. "That's the stupidest thing I've ever heard."

"One of my favorite sayings, son." Marty came through the front door just in time to catch Tanner's comment and note their proximity.

"Sorry, sir." Tanner dropped his hands from Julia's shoulders. Was he apologizing for the words or his closeness to her? The little wink he sent her way said the apology was totally word related. A trickle of joy made her dip her chin to hide her smile.

"Don't be," Marty said as he set down a tool-box. "It's one of those things farmers say because the work never ends."

"I do believe your son has mentioned that a number of times. And then he went and married a farmer."

"One of God's little ironies." Marty grabbed a face mask and looked around, impressed. "You guys aced this."

"Well, cleanup isn't going to be a fifteen-minute job," Julia noted, but she smiled at Tanner. "We discovered this is a great way to take out our angst."

"And a good way to bond," Tanner inserted, and when she looked up there was no mistaking the meaning in his eyes. He slanted her a smile and turned back to the wall. "But I've still got some work ahead of me, so if you'll excuse me…" He raised the hammer against what was left of the wall while Julia and Marty filled and dumped the wheelbarrow multiple times. By the time nine o'clock rolled around, they were a mess, but the room was now wide-open and all the debris had been swept out.

"Done. And exhausted." Julia tossed them their jackets and put hers on before she perched on the edge of a half wall. "I'm so glad I have tomorrow morning off. It will take that long to get this stuff out of my hair."

"You know when you add water to plaster dust, you get cement," Tanner said.

"No!"

Round-eyed, she stared up at him until he grinned. She muttered something under her breath but wasn't too upset with him as she stood. "Are the doctors in your practice *really* working construction here tomorrow night?" he asked in surprise. "I thought the grant money pretty much covered getting everything done."

"One of the grant requirements was to find volunteer labor for at least fifty percent of the project. It's not so easy to find volunteer labor these days, so I kind of hinted that the staff and their families would do it." She winced slightly. "A lot of our skilled retirees go south for the winter and won't be back until construction's complete, so I probably could have thought that part through a little better. Or asked for more time."

Marty chimed in. "By the way, if you're around Thursday morning, I'm buying lunch for anyone on hand. Julia's got an appointment first thing, but I know there's a couple of us showing up here to work. Laura and Tina could use some extra winter business at The Pelican's

Nest and there's always fresh lemon cream pie on Thursday."

"I'm available."

"Good!" Marty motioned to the door. "Are you two okay with locking up?"

"I've got it, Dad." Julia held up the keys. "Thank you for getting over here. We'd still be shoveling if you hadn't been able to make it."

"Maybe." Marty aimed a knowing look at the two of them as he moved outside. "Although you two seemed to have everything under control. See you Thursday, Tanner."

"Yes, sir."

"See you at home, Dad."

Julia followed Tanner out the door. He waited, blocking the wind, while she fumbled with the key. Between her tired hands and the dark night, something wasn't working right and she was just about to growl in frustration when Tanner's arms came around from behind her. "Let me help."

His hands took the key from hers and he slid it into the lock with careful deliberation. But it wasn't the key that had Julia's attention. It was the feel of his leather jacket beneath her cheek…the scent of sawdust…the rugged shoulders, sheltering her from the late winter wind.

Hope stole over her. She tried to fight the

emotion, but couldn't. It began in his gentle, strong manner and was nurtured by his serious gaze and his bright smile. He'd seemed downright prickly last week, but she saw none of that now.

But you did see it, so don't be fooled. People aren't always what they seem.

She'd found that out the hard way, but she didn't want to think of past mistakes. Not with Tanner so close. Tanner finished locking the door, dropped the key into her hand and tipped his gaze down from over her shoulder. "We're good."

Her breath caught, her eyes fixed on his, and when his gaze strayed to her mouth, mixed emotions fought for control. He put one broad, gentle hand to her cheek, then smiled. "It's cold out here. Let's head home."

They walked toward the parking lot together.

His words reminded her of old dreams gone awry. A home, filled with children and a set of loving parents. Was she shortsighted to think the dream could still exist? And if a woman was cast aside by one man, what were the odds she could build a lasting, loving relationship with another?

God has made all things beautiful in His time...

The pretty verse from Ecclesiastes gave her

a wake-up call. She put her hand on his sleeve. "Thank you. Thank you for not listening to me and coming to work anyway. And switching your meeting. And being really strong so I didn't have to do all the hammering."

He laughed. "My pleasure. See you Thursday."

"Yes." She got in her car and pulled away, oblivious to the fact that the car was cold, and the back window took a while to defrost properly, because she was going to see Tanner Reddington again in thirty-six hours. And that felt real good.

Dust-covered hair. Flecks on her glasses. Smudges on her cheek. Tanner had to resist the urge to gently rub the nail putty from Julia's skin. He held back, but just barely, and as she swung the door wider to let him in Thursday morning, her hand grazed his arm.

He offered the box of doughnuts as a diversionary tactic because she looked far too cute and sweet, and since he hadn't expected to see her first thing, it was more for his own peace of mind. "I figured sugar would make us work faster. And I thought you had an appointment."

Her eyes went wide. "It got changed to late afternoon." She frowned at the box of doughnuts, then brought her eyes back to his. "Thank you for the generous offer, but I think I'm going to pass for the moment. There's coffee around back."

"You brought a coffeemaker?" He set the doughnuts down, grabbed her shoulders and kissed her cheek. "Now we're talking. Although I wouldn't be opposed to getting us one of those fancy coffees from Tina's Café."

She looked taken aback. By the coffee talk or the impromptu kiss?

Tanner wasn't sure, but he peeled his jacket off, hung it out of the way and pulled the door open as Luke Campbell and Marty carried the saws in. They set up two staging areas on opposite ends. "Luke and I will work up here." Marty shoved a pencil behind his ear and kept his eyes trained on the line he was drawing. "You and Tanner can take the backsaw, Jules. You want to work on room one, two or three?"

"We'll do room one," Julia replied. "And I guarantee we can get it done quicker than you two."

Luke exchanged a look with Marty. "Is she serious?"

"Appears to be." Marty's dry voice gave no indication if that was good or bad. "Tanner, are you any good?" Marty arched a brow in his direction. "Because it appears your girl here just threw down the gauntlet."

"My girl? My construction partner, you mean?"

"His girl?"

Tanner's query had come out as a mild question. Julia's resembled a cartoon-style pterodactyl squawk, and that deepened her father's grin. "Let's see who's squawking at lunchtime."

Julia cut.

Tanner nailed.

The nail gun and saw didn't allow much conversation, but every now and again their eyes would meet...

And lock.

She blushed each time it happened, and he liked seeing the color rise in her cheeks, because then she'd make a face, as if warning him off. But five minutes later it would happen again.

Late morning, she raised a hand and called a halt. "Coffee, boys?"

"I'll make it." Luke finished nailing a two-by-six into place and headed around to the back.

Marty started to stretch but stopped short. "We've got company."

A woman stood just beyond the door, staring inside. Her loose coat flapped in the cold, wet, windswept day. She looked startled that they'd seen her, and turned away, but Julia was through the door in a flash, inviting her in, out of the cold. Tanner's protective side flared.

What was she thinking? She didn't know this woman. And neither did he and he worked this area all the time.

Midthirties. Disheveled. Brown hair, midlength, unwashed. Clothing in disarray. Old, worn, scuffed shoes and purse, a purse she hugged to her body as if protecting her life savings. She probably was. She glanced around, skittish, and when her eyes met Tanner's she shrunk back as if the intensity of his look unnerved her.

Luke came back into the room with two coffees and saw the new arrival. "Gracie Jayne? What are you doing down here? You okay?"

She looked half relieved and half embarrassed to see him, and Tanner felt like a slug for his instant rough assessment.

Luke crossed the room quickly. "What's happened?"

"My man's gone again." The rueful note in her voice said this wouldn't be a big surprise to Luke. "He won't be back this time because he met with trouble down I-95 and didn't make it through."

The look on Luke's face said he knew that Gracie Jayne's man—whoever he was—had died.

"I heard there was going to be a clinic for women here, and after all these years of never expecting anything, it seems I am." She opened her coat and the roundness of her belly underscored her words. "I think it should be soon, but I don't know for certain because it's never happened before."

"Have you seen a doctor?" Julia asked.

The woman shook her head.

"Then you've come to the right place." Julia's gentle tone and soft smile offered reassurance, but then she indicated the construction site with a wave of her hand. "We're not open here yet," Julia explained. "Can you come to my main office, Gracie Jayne? It's off Lower Lake Road, near Kirkwood."

Disappointment dulled the woman's features. She shook her head. "A friend brought me down the hill, and then the bus brought me to the edge of town. I walked the rest."

She'd walked almost a mile in this cold, drenching rain to find help, and there was none available. Sympathy welled inside Tanner, but it was cut short by Julia's brisk, friendly voice. "Well, I have a car and I'm not afraid to use it. Come on, I'll drive you over to the office. By the time you need a follow-up appointment, we'll be open here."

"You'd drive me?" Eyes wide, Gracie Jayne stared at Julia. "You wouldn't mind?"

"Why would I?" Julia grabbed her jacket as she spoke. She gave the men a look that said she was done for the morning, and opened the door. "When we're finished I'll bring you back to the bus stop or to your friend."

"But you have things to do." The woman looked around, as if wondering how Julia could just up and leave in the middle of the project. "Won't your boss get mad?"

"She *is* the boss, ma'am." Tanner aimed a respectful and encouraging look toward Julia. "We're just the hired hands."

"And this is what you do when you're not doing police work?" She peered up at Luke and he lifted his shoulders.

"It's always good to help a friend."

His words made Gracie Jayne smile. "It is. Well." She pulled the thin, large coat around her middle. "I'll be on, then. With…?" She looked toward Julia as she groped for a name.

Julia stuck out her hand in welcome. "I'm Julia Harrison, the midwife for the practice here."

As the woman's eyes widened in respect, Luke stepped forward. He handed the troubled woman a card. "Gracie Jayne, if you need anything, anything at all, you call me." He pointed to the base of the card. "My number's right there."

"I have it already." The admission seemed to make her uncomfortable. "From before."

"Well, that's all behind us now." Luke's gentle tone offered solace. "And there's room down here in the valley for you. You know that."

She made a face. "The thought of coming down doesn't look too easy after so many years of being up."

Tanner had learned the meaning behind her words his first year in Troop A. The back hills and mountains of the Southern Tier hid a fair share of secrets. He'd never patrolled the uplands, he'd been in the lake valley and Clearwater from the beginning, but Luke and his brother Seth had done mountain patrol for years. With lots of privacy and little access, twentieth-century stills had turned into twenty-first-century meth labs and drug rings. Part of the new task force's job was to shut them down, a daunting assignment. As soon as one shut down, another flared up on the next mountain over.

"I'll meet you guys later." Julia gave them a

brisk wave as she opened the door for her new patient. "One o'clock, okay?"

"One's fine."

Tanner faced Luke after they left. "Is she part of the mountain drug link?"

Luke shook his head. "No, but the man she used to live with was. Gracie Jayne is from a very nice family over in Olean, but she got mixed up with a loser in college, dropped out and decided to join a group of New Age hippies in the hills. That led to a drinking problem. She hooked up with Billy, and got herself on a wheel that never stopped turning long enough to break free. Maybe now that will happen."

"Is she still drinking? With a baby on the way?"

Luke shook his head. "She stopped about five years back, but never was able to reconnect with her family or friends. Her past embarrassed her and her family isn't the 'forgive and forget' sort."

Marty interrupted. "Tanner, you wanna work on our room or keep going on room one?"

"I'll keep going here." He gave each man a straight-on look. "But the race is off."

Luke laughed. "I suppose that's fair." He glanced toward the parking lot, and Tanner noted his concern.

"You worried about Grace or Julia?"

"Julia's pretty good at taking care of herself," Luke replied. "I'm concerned about Gracie Jayne," he admitted. "She didn't look right. And we never call her Grace," he went on. "Her parents called her Gracie Jayne and she kind of clings to that. So I never shorten it."

"Point taken," Tanner acknowledged.

"Pregnancy can take a lot out of a woman," Marty offered as he set the next two-by-six into place on room two. "Without good nutrition and medical help, well..." His face reflected the truth in his words. "It can be life-draining."

Life-draining.

Tanner weighed that expression as he bent over the saw at his end of the room. He'd never thought of having children in those terms. He'd assumed pregnancy to be a normal inconvenience, until everything went wrong in Ashley's sixth month, and then he was certain that someone had done something wrong. What if they hadn't? What if having babies wasn't as simple as he thought it should be?

The thought humbled him.

The sound of Marty's saw and Luke's hammer put him back in work mode, but he couldn't get Gracie Jayne's worried face out of his mind.

Something stirred inside him, a note of empathy wrapped in compassion. Another baby coming into imperfect surroundings. Usually that thought made him wince at what he'd already lost.

But today, something deep inside made him want everything to go well for the tired woman and her unborn child. He switched on the saw, and after ninety minutes of frenetic wall-building, he found he was only a couple of studs behind Luke and Marty. They combined forces and helped him finish off the joining wall between rooms one and two, then called it a morning.

Luke clapped Marty on the back as he grabbed his thick Buffalo-plaid flannel from a hook in the back alcove. "I've got to pass on lunch. I promised Rainey we'd have lunch together when I was done here, so I'm heading home. Great working with you guys." He shook Marty's hand, then Tanner's.

"Sure you don't want to tag along, Luke?" Marty asked. "I'm buying."

"Thanks, but no. Can't break a promise to the wife."

He strode off, humming, and climbed into his SUV.

Luke Campbell was living the American dream that eluded Tanner, but as he climbed into his car, he wasn't struck with the cumbersome, old weight of another man's good fortune, because the thought of gathering at The Pelican's Nest with Julia—and Marty, he inserted quickly—seemed too right to let old shadows darken it.

Chapter Six

Tanner turned north out of the parking lot, aimed for Kirkwood and pulled into the restaurant parking lot just ahead of Julia. Seeing her heightened his anticipation. He waited despite the cold, wet wind while she got out of her latest rental vehicle and walked toward him with a bright smile.

Something moved inside his chest. Her expression shone with joy, despite her wretched week and the ex-husband woes. She looked calm and happy, and seeing her joy made him want to feel the same way.

Calm down, Romeo. You're suing one midwife for malpractice and interested in another? Aren't you worried she's going to hate you when she finds out?

"How'd you guys do?" she asked him, her blue eyes bright and engaging, as if talking to him meant something. It dawned on him again that he *wanted* it to mean something.

"Rooms one and two are completely roughed in and ready for electric, plumbing and wall-board."

"Sweet!" She high-fived him and he realized he really wanted a hug, but she'd think him crazy, wouldn't she? "Let's grab a table. Dad's about to turn into the lot, and this wind is wicked. And try not to notice when he flirts with Laura, because he thinks he's being the most discreet man on the planet, which is, of course, laughable."

"Your dad and Laura?" Tanner looked across the half-full dining room, and sure enough, Laura D'Allesandro wasn't looking around the room. Her gaze was locked on the window, on the tall, broad-shouldered guy striding in from his farm truck, shoulders back, head high. "Gotcha."

"Uh-huh."

Julia's smile said she'd shared the secret carefully, knowing she could trust him and that made him feel even better.

"How'd everything go with Gracie Jayne?" he asked as they walked to an empty booth. The scent of sweet red sauce, grilled meat and something cinnamon-spiced made his stomach jump for joy. He hadn't realized how hungry he was until this moment. "Will she be okay?"

Julia wavered. "We'll be praying that baby to safety over the next few weeks."

"Something's wrong."

"I can't really say anything, but I've got concerns. Right now, I'm just thanking God that she came down the mountain to find us. A lot of the folks in the hills are so private that they deal with birth and death on their own, and no one ever hears a peep. This is better."

"You think it's still like that up there? I figured a lot of the stories I've heard are rural legend."

Julia slid into a booth and faced him. "I know it's like that. Hence the clinic. And the motto, One Woman, One Baby."

"Marty!" Laura D'Allesandro's surprised greeting interrupted their conversation, and cut through the noise of the busy lunchtime crowd, as if she hadn't watched his progress across the parking lot with eager eyes. "I'll be right over, Julia and Tanner are on the left."

"Wonderful." Marty's face lit up when she greeted him, and they exchanged smiles across the room, which said more than words ever could. "I'll be here waiting."

Color brightened her cheeks. Her smile deepened. "I'll be there soon."

Tanner looked at Julia. He grinned. So did she, but then she put her napkin on her lap, demure, while her father moved their way.

Marty slid into the booth next to Julia, nudged her over and gave Laura a hearty grin when she dropped off his coffee a minute later. "You know me well."

"I'm starting to." Laura smiled and set fresh cream on the table.

Their attraction threatened to interfere with lunch, but Julia took the matter in hand. "Laura, can I have a broiled chicken salad with Parmesan-peppercorn dressing, please, a diet soda and no bread."

Her father rolled his eyes. "You're absolutely beautiful, Julia. There's no reason in the world for you to go on a diet. Tell her, Laura."

"Why should I when you just did?"

"Which means I should stay out of things that aren't my business," Marty acknowledged.

"Right." Laura's smile softened her reply, and then she looked at Tanner. "The special, right? Rigatoni and meatballs with the famous Martinelli red sauce?"

"And leave room for the lemon pie Marty's had on his mind for the past two days," Tanner drawled.

He half expected Marty to look embarrassed or flustered, but instead, Marty smiled at Laura, and said, "The pie didn't have my full attention, of course."

Laura blushed. Julia's mouth dropped open. She hurried to close it and looked at Tanner.

He muttered, "Well done. I should be taking notes."

Marty winked at Laura, and as she hurried back to the counter area, he shifted his gaze to Tanner. "Wouldn't hurt you youngsters to learn from a seasoned veteran. Wasting time is generally in no one's best interests."

Julia burst out laughing. "Go, Dad!" She nudged his shoulder.

Marty shrugged as he stirred cream into the hot fragrant coffee. "At this stage of life, if God sees fit to send me a second chance, I'm old enough and smart enough to take it."

Marty didn't meet Tanner's eyes. He didn't have to. Tanner knew exactly what the older man was saying.

"Hey, guys." Tina came by to drop off waters and Julia's soda. "How's the clinic remodel coming?"

"Progress." Tanner uttered the single word as if it was the most wonderful thing in the world. "We have rooms."

"Awesome!" Tina grinned approval. "And just so you know, there's an extra lemon pie in the back I saved for my faves. Which would be you. And the entire Campbell clan, of course."

"Tanner and I have already staked our claim. Julia on the other hand…" Marty sent her a look that said she was being silly.

Julia shrugged him off. "I will allow myself one piece of pie on Sunday. That's my reward for eating healthy all week."

"I think you're being very sensible," Tina told her. She took a seat alongside Tanner for just a minute, and he had to slide over to give her space, which meant he was once again directly across from Julia's bright blue eyes, her pinned-up hair and the black-rimmed glasses tucked into the upsweep. She looked real good when she wore the glasses, sending knowing looks his way.

Without the glasses?

She looked simply beautiful, and the hair…

He wondered what it was like when she let it down. Curly? Wavy? Soft? Oh, yeah. He was 100 percent certain it would be soft.

"Thank you, Tina." Julia aimed a pert look in her father's direction. "At five foot four, I can't indulge in pie the way these six-footers can pack it away. And I don't want to wake up in five years and realize it's thirty pounds I need to lose instead of five or ten."

Tanner sent Julia a look that made sweet

color rise to her cheeks. "You think you need to lose weight, Julia?" When she started to stammer under the intensity of his gaze, he reached out, covered her hand with his and then squeezed gently. "Why would you think to improve on perfection?"

She stared at him as if gauging his sincerity, so he held her gaze, kept his hand right where it was and smiled.

Marty shot him a look of approval. Tina stood, grinned and went back to work.

Julia sat silent for long seconds, her eyes locked with his, until he gently removed his hand.

She breathed then, but the look on her face, as if he'd just sent her world into a spin, made him want to keep her world turning on a regular basis. And that felt real good.

He'd held her hand.

Julia tried to decipher the meaning behind Tanner's actions as she crossed the strip mall parking lot, but the sight of the smashed front window derailed her train of thought. She strode forward, furious, and when two hands gripped her shoulders and pulled her back toward the cars, she swung around, and almost punched Tanner in the jaw.

"Whoa, girl. It's me, one of the good guys."

He kept his voice low and kept backing her away from the shattered front window. "Stay put with your father while I check this out. Please."

She started to argue and Tanner gave her one of those "I know best" cop looks. He waited, silent, strong and crazy good-looking while she caught her breath. "Go ahead."

He moved forward, weapon drawn. The scream of a siren said he'd already called for backup, which meant he was able to assess things quickly because she hadn't noticed the broken glass until she was almost upon it.

You were thinking of hand-holding and long, slow looks. You'd do better to keep your mind on the tasks at hand. Dealing with Vic, this new clinic and keeping your boys happy. You don't need anything messing up your life right now, and a romance gone bad messes things up big time.

"Why would someone do this?" Marty stared at the broken window and ran a hand along the nape of his neck. "Who would be bothered by a women's clinic here?"

Tanner came back their way once he put his gun away. "Empty spaces make for easy meetings, drop-offs, pickups, handoffs. If the OB practice puts a successful site here, all of a sudden there's an increase in respectability.

In this area of Clearwater, that poses a threat to people who prefer to lurk in the shadows."

"You think they want to scare us off?"

Two sheriff's cars cruised into the lot, lights flashing. A state trooper SUV followed them in, and the gathered group of uniforms checked the premises thoroughly. "Nothing missing inside," Tanner reported when they came back out.

"All of your power tools are where they belong, but the brick throwers left you a message." The second trooper held up a scribbled note that had been wrapped around one of the bricks. "Do your good deeds somewhere else. Or else."

Julia stared at the threatening note. The hairs along her neck stood up. "They're trying to scare us out of here? That's the stupidest—" She pulled in a breath, moved forward and turned toward Tanner. "You warned me."

His expression said yes. His words offered something else. "Change for the better often starts in distress, Julia. In this neighborhood, when you ruffle one set of feathers, they turn around and ruffle the next set. And rarely is there an action that doesn't spur a reaction."

"It's not too late to change locations," Marty offered. "I like helping folks as much as the next guy, but the thought of you being in harm's way doesn't sit well, Jules."

"How do we reach the people who need us if we hide the clinic in an upscale suburban site, Dad? You saw for yourself that Gracie Jayne had to arrange a ride into the valley, then took a bus to the end of the line, then walked nearly a mile to access the clinic. If we put the clinic in some safe, antiseptic spot, we miss the intended outreach. You didn't raise me to do things halfway."

Marty scrubbed a hand to the base of his neck. "I might regret that particular mind-set about now."

The two deputies drew near. "Ms. Harrison, we're going to write up a report on this and we'll follow through with an investigation, but they're definitely warning you off. You might want to consider the possible repercussions of whatever decision you make. Like Trooper Reddington said, there's fallout just about anywhere in this area. Some of the locals get real worried about change."

"The decision's been made, and no brick-throwing idiot is going to mess up eight months of planning, grant writing and red-tape jumping." Spitting mad, Julia looked at Tanner. The expression on his face said he was sorry about what happened, but not surprised. "Can you guys keep us safe?"

"We can try. And once the clinic is here, the perps might shift their focus to another run-down area. There's no shortage of them for the next fourteen blocks."

"Which means it doesn't really matter which roughed-up area we pick, we could be targeted in any of them."

The second trooper nodded. "That about sums it up."

Julia pulled out her phone and called the same company that had boarded up her house a few days ago. "They're coming right out to board us up. I'm not going to have them re-place the window until the remodel is complete and we're in. Why give them another potential target? Once we're in, there will be an alarm system and cameras, so it might not be quite as easy to hit us as it was today. In broad daylight." She grabbed her father's hand. "Do you mind picking up the boys for me in a little while? I want to make sure everything gets done properly here."

"I'm not leaving you alone, I'm sure Piper—"

"I'm staying."

Tanner interrupted the conversation and his firm tone offered assurance, but he was supposed to visit Zach that afternoon. "You don't have to do that," Julia said. "You've done enough, so why don't you go visit Zach like you were going to do?"

"I'll visit Zach once we're done here." He kept his voice mild, as if he didn't have a life and things to do on his day off. "Right now, this is where I need to be. Zach would kill me if I left you here on your own. I'm staying."

"The boys have religion classes at the church right after school, so they don't need a ride for a while," Marty added. "I'll call Berto so that Piper can help with the afternoon milking and we'll be all set."

Julia stared at the broken glass. Emotions swelled within her. Anger, frustration and disappointment churned like thick, sour milk. How could something meant to bring good to a struggling community be perceived as a threat? The deputy sheriffs and the trooper had a quiet word with Tanner, then they all left. A few minutes later the emergency enclosure truck pulled up.

She didn't want to go inside the building and work, not knowing they were already a target, but she did, and Tanner followed behind her. She stopped inside the door. "You were right. I'm saying it now to get it out of the way, so you don't have to. This is a bad location, and maybe a bad idea all around."

In his face she saw more than just another law enforcement guy knowing too much. She saw a man who seemed to empathize with her, almost as if he understood her need to help, but that was silly because Tanner was single and lived in a yuppie-friendly condo overlooking the water on the more affluent part of the long, narrow lake. "It meant a lot to Gracie Jayne this morning."

That seemed like so very long ago, but he was right. It had meant a lot to the beleaguered woman.

"And it will mean a lot to others. Let's get a few things done, just enough so we don't leave here today feeling defeated."

"Why are you doing this?" She didn't mean to sound gruff, but she felt gruff right now, as if all of her good intentions were mired in calamitous results.

He pondered the question almost too long, then looked beyond her to the staked out rooms. "Because it might help someone who needs it. And right now, that's reason enough."

Julia moved ahead of him. All the midday thoughts of flirting and fun had been dashed by the vandalism, but when she pictured the day, Gracie Jayne's face was the image she carried into the work area. Nearly two hours later, when she'd finished framing the final two walls of room three with Tanner, the repeated physical pounding of the nail gun strengthened her resolve.

They'd have their clinic and they'd have it here, no matter what the local thugs thought. Because good care for women and unborn babies was what every one of them deserved.

For a guy who's made a practice of avoiding pregnancy like the plague, you're doomed, man.

Tanner shushed himself, knocked on Zach's door and pushed it open when he heard Zach holler from inside later that afternoon. He strode in and grabbed a seat next to Zach's recliner. "We need to come up with a plan to keep your sister safe."

"My dad filled me in," Zach acknowledged. "Knowing you were right won't thrill Julia because they'd already jumped headfirst into this project before she ran it by me a few months ago."

"And you told her what?" Tanner asked.

"Same thing you did. You mess with the locals, they're liable to make your life miserable. Now it will be our job, well—" he stared glumly at his raised leg "—*your* job to keep her safe. For the next few months anyway. You got any ideas who threw the brick?"

"Most likely someone from our cast of usual suspects, but we'll have to see how things pan out. Catching anyone will be hard unless we get footage. The clinic's security system won't go in for a couple of weeks when the electrician hardwires the place, so I'm installing a temp. I intend to have it in place by tomorrow night."

Tanner faced Zach more fully before asking the next question. "Was I wrong to tell Julia it was a bad spot? Because now I feel like a jerk for being right."

Zach shook his head. "You were spot-on, but Julia's brand of medicine is to take help to the streets as often as possible. Did you know she wrote the grant application for this endeavor?"

"Nope."

"Julia's got a heart of gold, an eager-to-please personality and a work ethic that puts most people to shame. That's why she and Piper get along so well. They're driven and bossy."

"And cute. And nice. And faith-filled." Piper came in from milking just in time to overhear Zach's words. "She's the kind of person who is constantly doing for others and expects nothing in return, and her ex-husband is a jerk for taking advantage of that."

"I can't believe she has to take the boys ninety minutes east next week to have her first face-to-face with the cheating moron." Zach's dark expression said he'd like to have a few words with Julia's ex-husband. "She won't let Dad go with them. My father's a peaceful guy, but he didn't take kindly to his only daughter being cheated on."

"She's got to take the boys across the state?"

"Vic lives in Ithaca. They're required to meet halfway between here and there."

"I'm going with her on the drop-off," Piper added. "But she's on her own for the pickup next Sunday, and Vic's the kind of lowlife that picks his moments carefully."

Any guy who took advantage of a woman like Julia was pond scum in Tanner's book. Tanner stood and moved to leave as Piper's stepmother bustled in the back door with Piper and Zach's boy, Jackson. The little guy spotted Tanner, shrieked in mortal terror and raced for his mother.

Tanner stood, rooted, not sure what to do because his simple presence scared the little guy to death.

Lucia moved in quickly. She started talking

to Jackson in a mixture of English and Spanish that defied mere mortal understanding. The toddler got the gist of her scolding. He peeked up and sent Tanner a smile so sweet and winsome that one side of Tanner's crusty heart melted while the other section shattered into a million pieces.

Solomon would have been eighteen months older than Jack. He'd never been given the chance to smile, laugh, run, jump, climb on counters and wreak havoc. So small and fragile, born too soon and gone just as quickly.

His heart cramped. He couldn't do this, couldn't stand here watching the blessing of Zach's beautiful child while missing his own. He started to leave, but then Jackson raced across the floor, grabbed hold of his legs and wouldn't let go.

Tanner froze. Should he pick him up? Talk to him? Or run for his life?

He looked down. Jackson's round eyes stared up at him, a blend of brown, green and gray like a winter sea. Tanner reached down, picked the little fellow up and hugged him.

And the toddler hugged him back.

Emotions rose high. His breath caught. He had to put the kid down and run because the onslaught of old feelings and lost chances grabbed him dead center and refused to let go.

He wasn't about to have an emotional break-down in front of these nice people.

He made a lame excuse to Piper and Zach, gently extricated Jackson's grip from his neck with Lucia's help and left as quickly as he could.

He got to his car just as his lawyer called. He hesitated, then answered the phone. "Darren, what's up?"

"We're on the brink of good news," the lawyer exclaimed. "Southern Erie Women's Medical will likely make an offer to settle out of court."

The news should have made Tanner feel better. Isn't that why he'd pursued the lawsuit? To make someone pay for the loss of his wife and child? "Why?"

"Lawsuits are costly," the lawyer explained. "They take a lot of time. Busy medical practices carry insurance for that very reason. For them to invest time in a suit they might lose makes no sense. So the insurance company seems willing to settle before we go to court, which is good, right?"

Was it? Tanner wasn't sure. "Does this admit their wrongdoing?"

"It doesn't have to," Darren explained. "It's a legal means to clear the case and move on, with significant payout to the injured party, which is you."

"So they're willing to pay me even if they think they did nothing wrong?"

"That's how the system works."

"Well, that's a horrible system, Darren." The lawyer's silence said Tanner's reply confused him, but then he launched what to him was probably a simple explanation.

"It makes things easier all around. They may not feel responsible for the sad outcome of your wife's heart problems, but they commiserate with your loss."

Tanner didn't want commiseration. He wanted justice. He wanted someone to admit they messed up and would never, ever do it again. He longed for the satisfaction of a heartfelt apology and a pledge to do better.

Instead, they were going to offer him money and clean their slate of him.

"There's no offer yet, and I'm not sure what time frame we're looking at, but I wanted to give you a heads-up. We're almost there, man. Almost there. The settlement's so close I can feel it!"

"Keep me updated," he said, then shut off the phone, afraid he'd say too much. Raw feelings wrestled inside him. Holding Jack Harrison, the scent and sight of the little boy so fresh in his mind—

What price could he put on that? None. He wasn't after money. He wanted justice. He wanted joy. He wanted—

He sighed, staring at the dank, dark, rain-shrouded March afternoon.

He wanted what he couldn't have. His family back. And no amount of settlement was going to fix that. Ever.

He hit Upper Lake Road and drove past Julia's boarded-up house. The reconstruction of her back wall and half the kitchen would take weeks. Then to have her new project targeted by vandals, in the midst of whatever was going on with her ex-husband, had to be the icing on the cake.

Growing up like he did, pulled in multiple directions by his parents, he hated divorce. He'd promised himself to steer clear of family drama. Been there, done that and had strong emotions because of it.

He wanted a normal family. Was that too much to ask?

He got home, parked, walked through the condo and stepped onto the balcony overlooking the water. Sheeting rain pummeled the strategically placed rock wall, built to keep water from flooding the western shore. Waves lapped the boulders, rising and falling beneath the condo lighting.

Lunch with Julia and Marty seemed like it'd happened years ago. He'd forgotten how nice it was to smile, laugh and talk with a woman. He'd dated a few times since Ashley's death, but it always seemed contrived and not quite right.

Until today, sitting in The Pelican's Nest, talking with Julia about her silly notion of dieting.

Julia, the midwife, a woman who pledged her life to helping other women, the very same profession he was suing for a great deal of money.

How could he reconcile it? And why did it feel wrong to push Ashley's medical practice for payment if they didn't do anything wrong? If they weren't negligent, why should they pay? Why *would* they pay?

Rain beat down on the gabled roof above him. It streamed along the shingles, blowing off the roof, missing the gutter about a quarter of the time.

Was it justice he wanted? Or was it revenge?

He leaned against the back wall of the balcony, watching water sluice from the sloping roof. He'd been so sure of himself and his actions two years before, a man on a mission.

Now, second thoughts gripped him. Should he walk away from the lawsuit or see it through?

He honestly had no idea which way to go.

Chapter Seven

Julia looked up from the papers her attorney Mike Silver handed her that afternoon and frowned. "There's nothing I can do except take the boys to their father next week?"

"Nothing that will do any good," he told her. "If it's a long, drawn-out custody battle you're seeking, they usually end badly and drag children through a whole lot of mud."

"I'd never do that."

Mike tapped the letter from Vic. "A fact he knows, I'm sure. So he's throwing his weight around, and we're going to go after him for his back child support. We can garnishee his wages if he doesn't come up with it within thirty days. He'll be mad about that, but if he's determined to have this part of the divorce decree followed, my guess is he knows better than to fight the financial aspects."

"I don't need his money," Julia asserted.

He shrugged that off. "Start a fund for the boys. College will be here before you know it. The fact is, their father should be providing some level of support. Kids are expensive, and footing the bill yourself hasn't prevented him from staking a claim now, has it?"

She shook her head.

"So we'll make it clear that he needs to follow all aspects of the divorce decree. Have you chosen a handoff point on I-86?"

"Alfred/Almond. There's a convenience store just off the expressway."

"I'll note that in our reply. Is six o'clock Friday okay?"

It wasn't okay but she nodded, because what else could she do? Didn't King Solomon favor the woman who tried to save her child from demise, the one who looked out for the boy's safety? She longed to be that kind of mother but she'd be lying if she ignored the misgivings grabbing hold of her heart. "I'll make it okay."

"Good." He stood and extended his hand. "I'm glad we're working together, Julia. It's been a pleasure to see you again."

"I appreciate your help," she admitted. "And I want to thank you again for seeing me so quickly. I didn't want to talk with Vic until I knew all my options." She shook his hand and smiled, and when he walked her to the outer door of the office, she thought she read a glimmer of interest in his eyes.

It's lack of food, most likely. The wry voice of her conscience really needed a muzzle, the sooner the better. *You always eat when you're anxious. Let's hit the drive-through on the way to the clinic.*

Let's not, she decided, and headed straight home.

She parked next to Tanner's car outside the clinic the following afternoon and nudged excitement aside. She stepped out of her car the same time he did, and when she met his gaze, her resolve melted into puddles at her feet.

Wearing a long-sleeved T-shirt and blue jeans, he came toward her, smiling, and that look of expectation grabbed hold of her heart and refused to let go. "I've got something for you."

"For me?"

"You and the boys." He held out his hand, clearly excited. "Tickets to the monster truck show in Orchard Park next weekend."

"Tanner. Thank you." She met his eyes with a look of regret. "I thought about getting tickets for the boys, but then realized they won't be here. They start their weekend visits with their father next weekend."

* * *

He read the disappointment in her voice, but Tanner read misgiving, too. The fact that a woman like Julia didn't trust the boys' father meant there was a good reason for it, because in the short time he'd known her, he'd figured out one thing. She was honest and upfront, the kind of person who inspired the faith of others.

He held the tickets up for her inspection. "It's for the final show, five o'clock on Sunday. What time do you pick up the boys?"

"Three o'clock."

"Where are you meeting them?"

She told him the location and he hit a few buttons on his phone. "It's only ninety minutes from there to the show, and it's an inside venue, guaranteeing loud noise, dirt and exhaust fumes."

She smiled up at him as she moved toward the door. "I'm so sorry to miss it."

"That's just it. We *don't* have to miss it."

"We? As in you and me?"

He held her gaze. "You, me and two boys who would love seeing the Extreme Dominator crush six cars in one monstrous sweep of terror."

Her hesitation made him press his point further. "I'll go with you to pick up the boys, we'll head to the show, it's over by seven and we drive back to Kirkwood. Boys are in bed a little late, but with great stories to tell their friends the next morning."

"Tanner, I—"

He sighed on purpose. "If it makes it easier for you to say yes, we can pretend it's not a date."

"Is it a date, Tanner?"

Was that doubt clouding the anticipation in her eyes? Suddenly he really wanted it to be a date. "Absolutely. I'll even buy the popcorn and slushies."

"My hero."

He threw her a quick grin as he took the key from her hand and opened the door. "Or a guy who's using cute kids as an excuse to see a monster truck rally. I've never been to one. And when I heard on the radio that the last show wasn't a sellout, I went online and got us really bad seats away from the action. Less dust to infiltrate our lungs that way."

She laughed, and it made him feel good to hear. "You don't mind driving with me to pick up the boys?"

"Not if it'll get me ninety minutes of quiet time with you." He peeled off his jacket, hung it on the hooks around back and moved to the saw at the far end of the newly formed hallway. "And it gives them a little transition time from going to Ithaca to see a dad they haven't seen in a long time—"

"Zach talks too much."

He shook his head as he withdrew the floor plan and then a two-by-six piece of wood. "Piper, actually, but she wasn't dishing dirt, she was singing your praises. My parents got divorced when I was a kid, the messy, long, convoluted kind. I figured a couple of hours of something completely different would end their weekend on an up note."

Silence reigned until he looked at her. She stared at him from the opposite end of the clinic, her expression saying she wasn't sure whether to laugh or cry. "I think you're right, and the boys will be out-of-their-heads excited."

"Good." He smiled at her across the work zone, and they stood there, smiling at one another for long, slow ticks of the old clock on the wall. "Well…"

"Yes."

He pulled his attention back to the wood as Marty strode through the door. Julia turned to greet her father, and if her greeting sounded a little more excited than usual, Tanner figured that wasn't a bad thing.

They were going on a date with two kids, a long drive, dust-filled air and really bad food, and he couldn't remember the last time he'd been this excited.

Pathetic?

Naw.

The thought of watching the enthusiastic oohs and aahs of two little boys felt downright good, and that was enough for the moment.

Julia scanned her Sunday morning checklist as her father walked through the door leading to the laundry room. "Dad, did you order the food for Zach's party today?"

"Yup." Marty ruffled Connor's hair and dropped a kiss on Martin's head as he moved through the kitchen. "I'm going to get cleaned up for church. We'll head over to Zach's to surprise him afterward. The food trays should get there around one."

"Perfect." Julia refilled the transparent frosting bag and set plastic jars of sprinkles in front of the excited boys. "But if he gets tired or is in too much pain," Julia cautioned as she finished topping two dozen cupcakes with blue-and-white swirled icing, "we leave."

"Yes, ma'am."

She sent her father a smile that apologized for being bossy and turned the boys loose on the cupcakes. Sprinkles went everywhere. She'd put a cookie sheet underneath the cupcakes to catch the excess, but a fair share of sprinkles bounced their way to the floor. Spike came around, tail wagging, licking the carpet as fast as he could.

"Spike likes sprinkles!" Connor laughed at the dog's happy expression as Spike lifted his gold-and-brown head, looking for extras. "Can I give him some?"

"He's had enough, I think." Coming home to a sick dog later wouldn't be fun for anyone.

Martin dropped his sprinkle shaker onto the floor, and when he bent to pick it up, a few clandestine shakes sent a fresh round of sprinkles scattering across the kitchen tiles. "Oops."

"He's like a vacuum cleaner," Connor breathed, watching as the sprinkles disappeared into the young mixed-breed overgrown pup. "And he loves them so much."

Julia grabbed up the sprinkles, capped them and tucked them away.

"Why is Titus so much better than Spike?" Martin wondered. Reverend Smith, their church pastor, had adopted Spike's littermate, one of the pups Zach rescued almost two years ago.

Connor threw an arm around Spike, then covered the dog's ears. "He's not one bit better, Martin! Spike's the best dog ever, he likes us so much and he always wags his tail."

Martin rolled his eyes in a look that said Connor was young and stupid. "Titus behaves better. He's always good. Reverend Smith can take him anywhere and he behaves. Spike's only good once in a while."

"You're a jerk!"

"No, you are!"

Connor clung more tightly to the wriggling dog as Julia closed the cupboard. "No one's a jerk, and if you keep acting like brats, you won't be eating cupcakes at Uncle Zach's birthday party later. Do I make myself clear?"

"Yes." Martin scowled at his younger brother and shoved his fists into the pockets of his pants. "I'm gonna go wait in the car."

"I'm gonna hug my dog." Connor stayed right where he was, whispering five-year-old comfort to Spike. The big pup sprawled onto the floor, then flipped, belly-up, hoping Connor would give him a belly rub.

Connor fulfilled the dog's wish, and when Julia called him to wash up for church, he sighed, then crossed to the kitchen sink. "Spike wants to be good."

Julia smiled. "Does he?"

"Yes. But he says it's hard sometimes."

"I expect it is," offered Marty as he came back into the kitchen, knotting his tie.

"You look wonderful, Dad."

He dipped his chin in acknowledgment and the sparkle in his eyes said he was trying to look good. "Thanks. Back at ya'. New dress?"

"Nope." She finished putting the lid on the cupcake tray. "It's one I didn't fit into for a few months. And now I do."

"Well, it's pretty."

"Thanks. Connor, you ready?"

He stared at Spike, called the dog's name and pointed to the big crate they'd brought from their house. "Go to bed, Spike."

The dog pretended not to hear. He looked right, then left, acting oblivious.

"Spike." Julia put a note of caution in her voice and the big puppy stood, rolled his shoulders and wandered into the crate, chin down. "Oh, you're breaking my heart, Spike."

Julia's offhand tone said the dog's antics weren't breaking her heart at all, but Connor's face said his angst was real. "I wish he would be good like Titus."

"Give him time, bud." Marty reached down and picked Connor up. "Let's get to church, and then we'll go pester Uncle Zach and make noise and tell him happy birthday and make him forget about his sore leg for a while. It doesn't hurt Spike one bit to be in the crate for a few hours."

"No?"

"Well, does it hurt you to be in bed at night?"

Connor shook his head. "'Course not."

"Well, this is Spike's bed. Dogs like to nap and lots of dogs nap in their crates. Makes sense, right?"

"It does."

Marty headed for the door. "We've got spring in the air today. I don't think he needs a jacket, do you?"

"Nah." Julia grabbed a lightweight sweater and the cupcakes, then followed them to the car.

Her boys missed out on a lot of that man-to-man interaction. They were blessed to have their grandpa nearby, and their uncle Zach, but the lack of a father left a big gap in their lives. Maybe Vic's timing would turn out to be beneficial. Maybe he truly wanted to be the father Martin and Connor deserved. Her prayer time today would be directed that way.

She climbed into the front seat of her dad's truck, determined to forge ahead, heart, mind and body, praying Vic had done the same. Which meant she might have to forgo a cupcake this afternoon, but knowing this dress finally fit right made her feel as if she was taking charge of her life again.

It felt good.

Chapter Eight

Drop-dead gorgeous.

Tanner couldn't hide the gleam of appreciation quick enough. When Julia spotted him at the far end of Zach and Piper's living room, the warmth in her cheeks said she caught his look…and knew exactly how much he liked the dress.

He started her way, determined to tell her how pretty she looked. Up close.

"Tanner, can you help Laura?"

Piper's request delayed his quest. "Of course. Where is she?"

"Coming in the front with the food trays."

"I've got it." Marty moved past them, swung the front door wide and handed off a large warm tray to Tanner. "If you guys wait inside the door, Laura and I can relay the trays to you. The warming racks are set up in the kitchen."

"Can do." Piper winked at Tanner. "How cute are they," she whispered as Marty cut across the grass in a hurry to help Laura. "Look how he rushes to help her. Zach, remember when we were like that?"

Tanner burst out laughing, and Zach managed a wan smile. "I'll be a hero again, I promise. Around June, just in time to plant the garden, mow the lawn, paint the eaves and seal the driveway."

"My poor baby." Piper leaned over and kissed him while Tanner accepted the next food tray from Zach's father. Julia appeared beside him and tried to take the tray into the kitchen. "I've got it." He kept a stubborn grip on the tray so nothing would mar the top of her dress.

"You sure?" She looked up at him and the Caribbean hues of her eyes put a lockdown on his heart. "I can carry this in while you get the next one."

"And ruin that pretty dress? Not going to happen." He grinned. "You look great, by the way."

A fleeting smile touched her face, as if she loved the words but couldn't quite trust them. "Thank you."

"You're welcome. And there's enough food here for an army."

"Which means a lot of leftovers," she whispered. "I think Dad wants to show Laura he supports the restaurant. Like, big-time."

"This'll do it." He ducked a little lower so she couldn't possibly miss his intent and said, "He does okay with this whole romance thing."

"Better than me," Julia muttered, and smiled when Tanner shoulder-nudged her. "Being out of practice is rough, because the rules have definitely changed in the past twelve years."

She was right. They had, Tanner realized. He motioned to the food. "Shall we start the line? We're here, the food's here and there's no mob scene."

"Kids first." Julia lifted a bunch of smaller plates. "Rainey, send the kids up here. Tanner and I will help them fill their plates."

"Excellent." Luke Campbell's wife turned their way as they pulled the lids off the food. Intense and inviting food scents poured forth. Chicken, Italian sausage with peppers and onions, barbecued beef...it was a feast for the eyes and the stomach.

Rainey Campbell turned pale and headed downstairs while sending her three kids up.

"Don't tell me. She's expecting, too," Tanner observed.

Julia nodded. "She's due just before Piper, and these adorable children," she drawled the words with full dramatic resonance, "are Zach's darling identical nieces Sonya and Dorrie…"

"I'm Dorrie and I wear purple," interrupted a little girl sporting a knowing look and a saucy smile. "Sonya's quiet and she wears pink. Unless we decide to swap just to mess everyone up." Dorrie gave Tanner a dazzling white smile against honey-toned skin. "And Aiden's our brother because our mom married his dad and now we're going to have a baby."

Clearly Tanner had no recourse around the Harrison/McKinney/Campbell crowds when it came to avoiding baby talk.

"We don't know if it's a girl or a boy," a blond boy about Martin's age explained. "Mom and Dad want to be surprised."

"Surprises are nice," Julia told him as she handed out plates. "You guys are big enough to know what you like and don't like, just don't waste food. Got it?"

"Got it!"

"Yes, Aunt Julia!"

"Tanner and I can help if you need it. We've got tables set up in the family room downstairs—"

"Can we eat outside, Mom?" Connor pleaded. "Grandpa moved the picnic table out of the garage with Uncle Luke, and it's really nice out today."

"And it will get six children out of the house," Luke stage-whispered to Julia. He held up six fingers and mouthed, "S-I-X."

Julia laughed. "Yeah, sure, soak up a nice day because they're rare in March."

Tanner kept a steady eye on the kids as they filled their plates, and they almost made it to the yard without a hitch, but Martin tripped at the edge of the stairs. He'd have tumbled head-long, but Tanner caught him before he hit the sidewalk. The paper plate, however, suffered a mortal blow. Pasta and chicken flew in multiple directions. Ripe black olives rolled down the sloping walk, and baby carrots landed in the grass.

Tanner kept his grip firm but light on the shaken boy. "You okay, Martin?"

The seven-year-old was trying not to cry. His lower lip trembled, his cheeks went tight and moisture pooled in his honey-brown eyes. He nodded, but when his gaze dropped to the far-reaching mess, one tear slipped down his pale cheek.

"If we only had a dog," Tanner remarked. "A dog would make short work of this clean-up for us."

Martin spun his way, surprised. "We have a

dog, but he's naughty. He's at Grandpa's house, in his crate because he doesn't behave."

Connor moved their way. "I thought he was in the crate because he needed a nap? That's what Grandpa said."

"You're too little to understand everything." Martin's superior tone said his level of comprehension stretched far beyond that of his younger brother. "I bet Titus doesn't have to spend every day locked in a big stupid crate. Our dog is dumb and doesn't listen."

"Is not!"

"Is, too."

"Is—"

"Guys, is your dog one of the puppies your uncle Zach found a couple of years ago?"

Martin waved toward the farm pond on the northern edge of the McKinneys' farmyard. "Right over there. They were in a sack and someone just threw them away."

Connor confirmed that with a nod, eyes wide. "Reverend Smith has one of the puppies, we have one and two other people took puppies, but Spike runs around a lot. And he kind of likes to chew things he's not a'sposed to."

Tanner stooped to their level, ignoring the mess around them for just a moment. "So Spike and Titus are brothers?"

"Yes."

"And brothers are always exactly alike, right? Like you two."

Martin stared at him, and then at Connor. "Except I like to read and play by myself and Connor likes to mess everything up and do 'Earth-shake' and then doesn't want to clean things up when he's done."

"So, you're different."

Connor nodded. "A lot."

Martin shrugged. "Yeah. I guess."

"Titus and Spike are different, too," Tanner explained. "Just because they're littermates doesn't mean they're going to act alike or do the same things or even grow up the same way. Do you think Reverend Smith gets down on the floor and wrestles with Titus?"

Connor burst out laughing. "I don't think he'd do that ever!"

Martin answered quietly, "He probably just sits and pets him. And takes him for walks."

"You guys have a big fenced yard so Spike can run free whenever he wants," Tanner continued. "Reverend Smith has a small rectory yard and a big cemetery behind him, so Titus can't jump and play all the time. His family life is different."

"So Spike isn't dumb?" The hopeful note in Connor's voice made Martin roll his eyes, but when Tanner answered, Martin's expression softened.

"No, not at all. He's different, just like you and your brother are different. He'll settle down after a while, and turn into a nice dog, but it's kind of cool for Spike to have two big strong guys to play with and take care of him."

Connor gulped, guilty. "Mom does most of that, actually."

"She does, but she'd love more help." Julia stepped through the door behind them, and the look of gratitude she shot Tanner said his explanation had been overheard.

He moved to give her room to come down the steps. She bent closer to Martin as she handed him a fresh plate of food. "Go eat with your cousins. We'll clean up this mess."

"You sure?" He looked up at her, and while he didn't look like Julia, Tanner sensed he had that same anxious-to-please personality. "I don't mind helping, Mom."

"I appreciate that, but Tanner's right. If Spike was here, he'd have cleaned all of this up already. As it is, I've got a broom and I'm not afraid to use it."

"Thanks, Mom." Martin flashed her a grin, grabbed the new plate with two hands and rushed to the picnic table set in the middle of the sun-soaked yard.

Connor turned to go, but then he turned right back and gazed up at Tanner. "You should come to our house and play with Spike. I think he would like you a whole lot, Mr. Tanner."

"That's a great idea, Connor. I like playing with dogs."

"Do you have a dog?"

Tanner shook his head. "Nope."

"Do you have a little boy like me?"

Tanner's heart chugged to a slow, painful stop, but after taking a deep breath, he stooped low again. "I don't. But I would be very proud to have a little boy like you or Martin. Go eat. I'll come to your house and play with Spike sometime soon, okay?"

"Okay!" Connor dashed off, then waved from the table, as if almost too excited about Tanner's visit to worry about something as mundane as food.

"You've gone and done it now." Julia handed him the dustpan while she swept as much of the food as she could into the plastic base. "He won't let you forget that you promised to come play."

"I don't want to forget it, just so we're clear."

She slanted him a look of doubt. "I'm a single mother, Tanner, and that means I keep my risk level with the boys aimed straight at the 'nonexistent' setting."

"Less excitement that way."

"And less cause for regret." She reached for the dustpan while he reached for the broom.

He took the broom and kept the dustpan and walked around the sidewalk to the garbage tote in the garage, hoping she'd follow.

She did. "I could have done this."

"I know that, Miss Independence." He smiled down at her once he'd disposed of the fallen food. "And I can't believe I'm saying this, but I kind of like that independent streak and that surprises me a little."

"Welcome to the new millennium, Tanner."

He laughed, set the broom and dustpan inside the garage and slung an arm around her shoulders. "It's not that. I love the idea of women being self-sufficient and earning money and having careers. But not too many women I know can raise kids, operate a power saw, deliver babies, write grants and look this good." He smiled down at her, and when she smiled back, all he wanted to do was lean in and kiss her. Just to see if kissing Julia would be as wonderful as he thought it would be.

"Are you going to kiss my mom?"

Shrieks of laughter followed Connor's loud question, so Tanner ducked his head, swept a sweet, quick kiss to Julia's very surprised mouth and turned to the tableful of children. "It appears so."

Giggles, laughs and a chorus of "eews" filled the air.

Julia ducked her head, muttering to Tanner, "You're a troublemaker. You're going to get all the little bees and a few big bees buzzing. And I've got no time to deal with cute state troopers with chips on their shoulders."

Her smile softened the warning, and the thought of kissing her again, without an audience, made Tanner take a half step forward. "Cute? You think I'm cute?" He gave her a lopsided grin. "And what if the chip on my shoulder managed to disappear? What then, Julia?" He whispered the last, then gave her hand a private little squeeze. He walked over to the table full of loud, goofy kids and sat down in the middle of them.

He'd spent so much time avoiding life, that to be suddenly plunked into the middle of the huge, sprawling clan felt almost good and normal. Like he was living and breathing on his own again.

He looked back toward Julia.

She looked intrigued, perplexed and possibly smitten. A beautiful woman, surrounded by love, life and laughter. This was the dream he'd longed for years ago, the dream he'd lost.

Could he find it again? Did he dare?

"Hey, Tanner! Do you like seafood?"

He scolded Dorrie with a quick look. "If your mother sees you chewing with your mouth open, she's not going to be happy. And besides." He ruffled her hair. "That's the oldest joke in the book, kid. Get some new material, will ya'?"

Dorrie laughed. Sonya sent a shy smile his way, a softened mirror image of her more boisterous sister. Aiden and Martin were deep in conversation about some new kind of remote control airplane club starting up on the west shore, and Connor was stuffing pasta into a napkin and trying to hide it in his lap. Tanner leaned his way. "You don't like the pasta?"

"I love it." Excitement marked his face. "It's one of my most favorites."

"Then why hide it?" Tanner tipped a finger to the rolled napkin on Connor's lap.

"For Beansy," Connor whispered. "I like to take Beansy and Miss Daisy treats. Maybe Miss Daisy will have her babies today, and she'll need all the energy she can get because Mom says having babies is real hard work."

"It is." Tanner put his mouth to Connor's

left ear and kept his voice soft. "Shall we go check on Beansy and Miss Daisy when you're done? Together?"

"Oh, yes!" Connor turned, knocked Tanner in the chin with a fairly bony head for such a little kid, then stopped, chagrined. "I didn't mean to hit you, Mr. Tanner! Here, let me rub it for you. Rubbing it makes it better." Connor proceeded to rub Tanner's cheek with sticky, greasy, little boy fingers, and his intense expression said he truly wanted to help ease his friend's pain.

Another rusty knot fell loose from Tanner's heart. The boy's quick care said Connor had a gentle heart despite his rambunctious nature.

"Is it better now?"

Anxious blue eyes peered up at him. Tanner nodded and gave Connor a quick hug. "So much better."

"Good!" Connor waited until the other kids were done with their food. Once they were taking their plates back inside, he slid off the end of the picnic table bench. "If we go now, we can give them their treat and be back in no time."

"Shouldn't we tell Mom?"

"If we do, then all the kids will want to come and Mom said it's not good for Miss Daisy to get too excited right now, that she needs some peace and quiet." He looked worried that too many kids would spoil the adventure.

Tanner nodded in agreement. "Sound advice."

"And as long as I'm with a grown-up, we're okay."

Tanner was pretty sure a mom would want to know where her kid was even if it was with another grown-up, so he texted Julia a quick message and took Connor's hand. "Lead the way, bud."

"I will!"

They strode across the backyard, cut through a small field and then walked over the small bridge Zach and Marty erected over a drainage ditch that separated the original McKinney Farm from Zach's property.

"Here's where they live!" Connor crept forward on tiptoe feet, watching. Peering.

Beansy came to the edge of his pen quickly, begging. Connor slipped the Nigerian dwarf goat a treat, then moved to the other pen, set against the barn's edge, about fifteen feet away. He looked inside, and frowned. "She's not here. But it's a nice, sunny day and she likes to be outside on nice, sunny days, Mr. Tanner."

"Shall we check inside the barn?" The goats had a small hatch cut into the barn wall, so they could move inside during rough weather spells. The minute he and Connor got into the barn, Tanner sensed trouble. The little doe wasn't curled up, lazily awaiting picture-perfect childbirth. She was pacing the small pen, mounding fresh straw, then straining with all her might, but nothing came of her ardent endeavors.

"Is she okay?"

"I'm sure she is." He wasn't at all sure, so he pulled out his cell phone and hit Julia's number. "I need you and Piper to assess the situation in the barn ASAP, okay?"

Her return tone said she heard what he didn't dare say in front of Connor. "We'll be right there."

"Is something wrong?" Connor gripped Tanner's hand, gripped it tight as minutes ticked by. "Is Miss Daisy in trouble?"

He didn't know. He couldn't tell if she was in trouble or if he was simply overreacting to a perfectly normal situation. How would he know? He'd never had the experience of seeing a child born, or a goat or even a puppy for that matter. He hunched low, but couldn't stop the anxiety welling up inside him. "I'm not sure what's normal for goats having babies, so I called Mom and Aunt Piper. They should be right here."

The two women came in through the barn

door together. Julia had ditched the dress and donned someone's sweats. Their breathing said they'd run across the field, and as they approached the doe's pen, Miss Daisy labored through another contraction. Tanner couldn't bear to look into the doe's eyes, the worry and stress of what might happen reflected in the 'help me' expression on the animal's face.

"Julia, I've got my birthing kit right there."

Julia pulled down a wrapped parcel from a shelf above the pen. She opened the bundle and knelt in the straw alongside Piper. "Coach me as needed."

"Will do." Piper examined the goat and frowned. "We've got one crosswise, blocking the birth canal."

"Can you shift it?"

"Hopefully."

Hopefully? Tanner's heart started beating harder in his chest. What did she mean, hopefully? If she couldn't do the job, shouldn't they call the vet? And should he stay there with Connor or take the kid away? "Should we go?" He asked the question softly, not wanting to cause the stressed animal any further duress, but at that moment, Miss Daisy appeared more interested in Piper's help than the presence of a stranger.

"I want to stay." Connor's tone and expression implored. "Miss Daisy loves me and she knows I love her. Mom, can I stay, please?"

Julia kept her eyes on Piper's intervention as she answered. "Connor, we talked about this, remember? That sometimes everything goes fine when a baby animal is born, but sometimes it doesn't."

"But we'll do our best, won't we?" His voice was soft, but the end of the question pitched up significantly.

"We always do," Julia assured him.

Her words stabbed Tanner in the gut. Maybe Julia always did her best, and maybe midwives were good at their jobs, but when things got dicey, shouldn't they call for help? Like now? "Should we call the vet?" He pulled his cell phone out of his back pocket. "We can get Miss Daisy to the clinic in ten minutes."

Piper shook her head. "No time for that. If I can just get hold of this baby's head—"

Tanner couldn't listen to any more. He let go of Connor's hand and strode out of the barn, across the yard and to his car.

His heart rate soared. His gut clenched. His breathing accelerated, and he was pretty sure he was on the verge of a full-fledged panic attack.

Nerves tightened his belly, and he was glad he hadn't taken time to eat. He got into his car, backed out of the driveway, and drove as far and fast as he could before he had to pull off to the side of the road and get sick.

The sight of Piper, sprawled on the barn floor, trying to help the laboring animal, had hit him square between the eyes. Why didn't she call the vet at the first sign of trouble? Why did untrained people think they could save the day when there were trained professionals nearby?

He sank to the ground next to his car, trying to rein in his emotions. The image of an unskilled farmer trying to save a few dollars while the animal suffered made him physically ill and just plain angry.

His cell phone buzzed.

He ignored it.

It buzzed again a few minutes later. He pulled it out, saw it was a text from Julia, and read the message. You okay?

He wasn't okay, none of this was okay, and he couldn't stand there and pretend it was all right to let people play doctor.

He didn't answer, he didn't have the strength to answer, but a minute later, a picture came through, a picture that made him stop and stare at the small screen.

Connor and Piper flanking the back of Miss Daisy's pen, and beside Miss Daisy were three pretty little kids, two brown-and-white baby does and one black-and-white-spotted fellow.

And her caption?

Success! Two doelings and a little buck, adorable and all okay! Thanks for calling us in, you saved their lives!

Emotions swamped him.

He saved their lives by making a phone call?

And then you ran away.

He sighed, leaned his back against the solid support of his car and replayed the past thirty minutes in his head.

He'd taken off in a time of trouble. He'd run scared by the probable outcome, and he'd been 100 percent wrong. What kind of person did that? What kind of *cop* did that?

Clouds moved in, stealing the transient warmth of the late winter sun, and with the clouds came a brisk, chill wind, the kind that said winter hadn't finished with them yet.

He stayed huddled against the car, getting cold, unsure what to do, but then Connor's words came back to him, from the day they first met. *Every day I pray and pray for these babies, and she hasn't had them yet.*

Something moved inside him. Something cold and hard and unyielding came loose when he pictured the boy's earnestness. The wind came stronger, a steady push of bone-chilling air, and still he sat, staring up into the heavens. "You want me to pray? Is that it? I should look up and assume You're there, listening? Because I don't believe it. I don't think I even want to believe it because I know how unlikely it is. I'm not stupid."

Drops of rain fell, then paused. The wind increased, and the trees lining the road's edge rubbed together, whining.

His phone buzzed one more time, and he almost threw it. He knew Julia must think he was weak to run off when things got tough. It was what he thought of himself right now, but when he looked at the text, it wasn't from Julia.

It was from his sister, Neda. He'd ignored her phone calls at the beginning of the month. He hadn't wanted her sympathy or her gentle wisdom. Right then, he'd just wanted to be left alone.

And then circumstances had bombarded him with pregnant women, a women's clinic, a laboring goat and a tableful of beautiful children, everything he'd avoided for years.

He opened her text.

Love you. Miss you. Praying for you every single day. God bless you, big brother.

His heart went tight again.

Neda was a wonderful woman. She'd been a great sister growing up, and he stood up at her wedding six years before. Now she had two beautiful kids, and he'd shied away from her and her growing family because he was protecting himself.

He felt selfish and stupid all of a sudden. And lonely. And cold and wet as the rain started to beat down harder.

He stood, rounded the hood of his car and settled into the front seat. He turned the key, switched on the heat and let the fan warm him.

Praying for you every single day. God bless you, big brother.

He'd let her down. He'd let himself down. And today, he let Julia and Connor down. He drove past the sweet white clapboard church where Reverend Smith and Titus spent their days, past the cute stores lining Main Street, and past the town park overlooking Kirkwood Lake. He didn't look up, toward McKinney Farm, he didn't go back to see the three new baby goats and come face-to-face with what a jerk he'd been.

He headed for the privacy of his condo, where a guy could be left alone with preseason baseball and a cup of fresh, hot coffee, no risk involved. Julia thought he had a chip on his shoulder. That he was a high risk.

She was wrong.

He was in the no-risk zone, and he was pretty sure he should stay there if something as simple as goat babies sent him over the edge.

He was ashamed of himself, not just for the whole barn incident, but for leaving his sister to fend for herself. He'd shrugged off his little niece and nephew, as if his grief was more important than Neda's joy. He'd been carrying a rock-hard grudge like a badge of honor.

Are you getting this finally?

His conscience gave him an extra smack for good measure as he walked into his empty upscale apartment and switched on the television.

Everybody got their share of hard hits, but then they moved on. It was time for him to wake up and smell the roses. He liked being in the middle of those kids today. He liked being with Julia, hanging with the family. He acted normal—

Until you didn't.

The mental scolding hit home.

The seventh-inning stretch came on the preseason game, and the chords of "God Bless America" rang through his living room.

He wanted to believe. A part of him longed to believe there was something bigger and better than him out there, but he'd been wanting proof for a long time, and none came.

Or so he'd thought.

He grabbed his phone and called Julia's number.

"Hello, Tanner." She didn't sound mad, she sounded understanding. Sympathetic. And slightly amused. "So I'm guessing you haven't had a lot of birthing experiences in your life, right?"

She thought he'd run out because birthing was a messy process. If only that was the case... "I called to apologize."

"No need!" She laughed, and he knew she was laughing at him because she thought he was just another squeamish guy. "All's well that ends well and the babies are doing fine, Connor is a proud uncle and Miss Daisy is pretty sure she's the best mom ever."

"Good." He didn't know what else to say, because he'd expected to be reamed out, but then, this was Julia. She was tough when necessary, but her gentle nature took precedence. And he loved that about her. "I'm on duty the next three days, but I can help at the clinic on Thursday afternoon."

"That would be wonderful. And thanks so much for taking time with Connor and Martin today, Tanner. It meant a lot to them."

"To me, too."

Seconds ticked by, as if she didn't really want to hang up. Neither did he, but he wondered what she'd think of him if she knew the real reason he'd run away.

For the moment, he'd let her think he was just another guy with a queasy stomach and let it go at that.

"So…Thursday. Should I bring doughnuts?"

"No." Her voice firmed quickly. "I've been doing so well, I'm determined to keep up my new healthy choices thing. With my weird schedule, it's time I started taking simple healthy precautions more seriously."

"You're beautiful, Julia. Just the way you are."

She drew in a light breath, and he wondered if she was reaching up, touching her hair, twisting one of the escaped locks around her finger like he'd seen her do before. And was she wearing her glasses or were they tucked into her hair? "Thank you. You're not so bad yourself, Mr. Tanner."

Her sweet reply made him smile, and using Connor's nickname for him seemed right. "Can I buy you supper after we're done on Thursday? Take a pretty lady out for a low-carb meal?"

She laughed out loud, which made the

cranky wheels of his heart turn easier again. "Not that night. I have to get stuff ready for the boys' trip to Ithaca on Friday. And you're still sure Sunday is okay? To drive to Alfred with me and pick them up?"

"Followed by two hours of dirt, dust and mayhem, yes. I'm bringing earplugs for all of us."

"I won't say no to that." She paused slightly, then said, "Thanks again, Tanner. For everything. See you Thursday."

Her thanks humbled him. She had no idea why he ran out on her today. She didn't know what he truly thought about her profession, and she'd probably hate him when the truth came out. That meant he needed to tell her the truth. He needed to take charge of the situation.

Would she understand his actions? He didn't know, but he needed to take the risk. Julia had dealt with a dishonest man once. There was no reason why she should ever have to deal with that again.

Chapter Nine

"Tanner, you made it." Marty's welcome at the front door was loud and clear.

Julia didn't look right away. Seeming too anxious was in no one's best interests, and knowing Tanner had come to help made her feel good. First she finished the coat of primer she was rolling on room one's back wall, then turned.

He was watching for her. Waiting. That realization sent her heart tripping into a sweet pattern, and when he reached up and tipped his baseball cap, ever so slightly?

She melted.

He moved her way, eyes locked on hers, and when he got to the enclosed room and the fresh paint, he whistled lightly in appreciation. "Nice job. It's getting there."

"It is. I love it," she confessed. "Sue, come here. Meet Zach's replacement."

Dr. Salinas came their way and stuck out her hand. "Sue Salinas, nice to meet you. You're Tanner Reddington?"

He tossed Julia a quick questioning glance. "You've been discussing me?"

"I may have told Sue what a help you've been to us here."

"We're grateful." Sue pulled her hair into a ponytail and pointed to the calendar on the wall. "We want this up and running, ready for a post-Easter opening. We're already fielding calls at the main office from people interested in using the clinic, so word's getting out."

"Can they come to the main office in the meantime?"

"They could," Julia replied, "but a lot of these women are in rough circumstances. If we send them to the more upscale environment of the main office, it can make them feel uncomfortable. And then they don't come back."

"When this is done, it will have all the amenities of the main office, but the simplicity of a health clinic," Sue added. "That way scuffed-up shoes, worn purses and thin-seamed clothes don't stand out."

"You've given this a great deal of thought. And I expect Julia shared my misgivings about the location with you."

"You're among friends when it comes to that

advice." Sue laughed. "We've taken our share of heat about this spot, and the brick-throwing incident bears that out, but if we're afraid to go to the streets, how do we expect to help the people in the streets?"

"It's a noble gesture," Tanner agreed.

"Not noble." She downplayed that quickly. "Inspired. Miranda, Julia and I all prayed, and after about six months of putting it in God's hands, this property came to us via the former owner. He donated it for the sum of the back taxes, which were paid by donations, leaving the grant money for the rebuild. I think God's hand has been on every inch of this project, and I pray every day that we can do it justice."

He glanced from one to the other. "Who's Miranda?"

"Dr. Matthews," Julia told him as she tapped the paint can cap into place. "She's the third corner of our busy triangle." She set the can of primer down and stood.

Mixed emotions marked Tanner's expression. Julia poked his arm in a friendly gesture. "We are guaranteed to fail at one hundred percent of the chances we don't take. Hopefully this will all work out and the clinic will run peacefully as long as it's needed."

"True enough." He agreed in word, but his

expression looked aggrieved and Julia didn't know why.

Sue's cell phone rang. She scanned the call display and faced Julia more fully. "It's Southern Erie Women's Medical. I'm on their expert witness list if a current malpractice suit goes to trial, so I have to take this, and then I'll be at the office."

"Okay. Tanner." Julia faced him, but paused. "What's wrong? Are you okay? I promise there are no goats giving birth today. You have my word on it."

He frowned. "And again, I'm sorry about that. It was the wrong thing to do."

"Oh, please." Julia shrugged it off and went back to work. "Do you want to do primer on room two or help with the ceiling?"

"I'll paint."

"Good." She handed him a tray and roller setup and added, "Dad did all the cutting in with the brush, so this part is pretty easy."

"Right." He took the tools into the adjoining room and set to work rolling primer onto the new wallboard. He didn't talk, he didn't whistle, he just walked away, and when he did, Julia's fairy-tale hope of something new and wonderful growing from their friendship fizzled.

She'd been unable to make Vic happy for

years. Despite her efforts, she'd never been able to inspire the true warmth and joy a good marriage maintained through the falls and foibles of real life.

She was not about to chance that again, ever. Never again would she jump through hoops to meet someone else's needs. They'd either accept her for the person she was, the person God made her to be...

Or she'd kick them to the curb. And right now?

Tanner's feet were on the edge of the road, pointing out.

Dr. Miranda Matthews was part of Julia's practice here.

How could that be? Her name was on the list of defendants in his lawsuit as a practitioner for Ashley's OB practice. He'd never met her, he'd only met two members of the staff during Ashley's months with them, but he remembered the name. And Julia's other colleague was being called as an expert witness? Was it coincidence? Common practice?

He had no idea, but the look on the doctor's face said she'd do what she had to do.

Were they in collusion? Did doctors cover up for one another to avoid hefty payouts? Or was she sincerely invested in the best medical care for women?

He rolled primer with a vengeance, got room two done and moved to room three without being asked, and by the end of the afternoon, the three exam rooms and the access hall and blood-draw alcove were primed, as well. He'd done it all without saying a word, so when he discovered Julia had left twenty minutes earlier, he felt like a jerk.

He pulled out his cell phone and almost hit her number, then realized he had nothing to say. How could he confess that he might be the reason Dr. Salinas was being called to testify on behalf of Southern Erie Women's Medical? He repocketed the phone and moved toward the door.

"Tanner."

He turned and waited for Marty to catch up.

"Nice job today, but somewhat quiet. You okay?"

He wasn't, but he wasn't going to talk about it, especially not to Julia's father. "Fine, thanks."

"That was believable." Marty's expression indicated it wasn't the least bit convincing. "You know, when my wife was killed in a car accident, I figured my world was over. We lost a son a long time before, a little boy named

Cameron, and that changed me. I wasn't my-self. I was there in body, but not in spirit, and it showed." He turned the key in the lock, tested the door, then resumed his side of the one-sided conversation.

"I pretty much left Janet to be the caretaker of our kids, so I didn't have the relationship with them I do now. Once Cam was gone, I got so involved in being the best at everything I did, that I forgot to just sit back and be still. And then Janet was killed, and I didn't think I wanted to live because everything, and I mean everything, was just plain empty. Who wants to live like that?"

Tanner didn't move. No one here knew about Ashley, did they? Except Alex Steele.

"Then I got sick," Marty continued. "They thought I had Alzheimer's, the early kind that messes you up quickly. I couldn't function on my own and they put me in a nursing home. Sold everything I worked so hard to earn. And I remember being trapped in that body and thinking if this ever gets better, I'm going to be the best father, the best grandpa and the best person I know how to be."

"You recovered?"

Marty stared straight at him. "I recovered because I didn't have Alzheimer's. A smart doctor here realized I'd been misdiagnosed and getting the wrong treatment for over two years. I lost my farm, my home and woke up to a totally different existence. It took me a while to get used to things, that's for sure."

"They messed up your diagnosis?"

"To the max."

"And are you suing them?"

Marty's look of wisdom said more than his words. "No. And I don't intend to, either."

"Why?" Tanner held his gaze, because either Marty was the nicest guy in the world or fairly stupid, and he'd gotten to know the older man recently. There wasn't anything dull-witted about Marty Harrison.

Marty ignored the stinging late-season snowflakes and the sharp west wind. "Mistakes happen. They weren't deliberately trying to mess up my life, and in the end I learned the most valuable lesson there is—to put my family first. This way I'm here to help Piper develop McKinney Farm to its full potential, I get to help raise my grandchildren and I'm not too old to start all over again, it seems." He flashed a smile and a wave over Tanner's shoulder, and Tanner didn't have to look to know Laura had just pulled into the pock-marked parking lot in front of the women's clinic. "But it took me a while to get my head in the game."

Tanner wanted to know why Marty sought

him out and told him all this. Did Marty know
what happened? And if so, how? He started
to ask, but Marty held up a hand that said he
didn't need to. "I did a Google search, son.
Doesn't take much these days to find things
out if you've got reason to look, and I saw
the way you were looking at my daughter last
week."

Tanner flushed.

"She's been through a lot, and I'm not interested in seeing her deal with another broken
heart in this lifetime, so you need to tell her
what's gone on with you, Tanner." His rock-
hard gaze said he knew Tanner's secrets. "Julia
deserves nothing less than your honesty. And
it's up to you to make sure she gets it."

Marty turned to go, then swung back, fac-
ing Tanner again. "Don't break her heart. You
might be a quarter-century younger, but I've
been runnin' and ridin' herd a long time. I've
got a few go-rounds in me yet."

"I won't, sir. I promise."

"See that you don't." Marty moved to Laura's
car, climbed into the front passenger seat, and
made no hesitation about leaning over and giving her a kiss.

Words of wisdom. Sage advice.

He thought he'd be upset that someone
knew the truth he'd tried so hard to put behind

him, but the minute he read the sympathy in Marty's eyes, he felt better. More normal.

Was he stupid for locking so much up?

Probably.

And foolish for wanting justice served?

He'd gotten an email from the attorney's office earlier that day, another hopeful post about a settlement. Only Tanner didn't feel triumphant. He felt guilty.

He trudged to his car, started to climb in, but a familiar voice stopped him. He turned and saw Gracie Jayne moving his way. She didn't look good, and her awkward movements said the woman needed help, quickly.

He grabbed his cell and called for an ambulance.

She stumbled toward him. Drunk? Drugged? While she was expecting a child?

He hoped not. He prayed not. When he saw her color under the thin yellow glow from the few unbroken lights above, the gray cast to her skin grabbed him, heart and soul. He took gentle hold of her arm and eased her into his backseat. "Gracie Jayne, you hang on, okay? Help's coming."

"Is she here?" Gracie Jayne's tired gaze flicked to the worn building and the boarded-up window. "Miss Julia. Is she here?"

"I'll call her." He hit Julia's number, and

prayed for the second time in three minutes, and when Julia answered on the third ring he thanked God again. "Julia, I'm in the parking lot of the clinic with Gracie Jayne. I've called an ambulance to transport her and she's asking for you."

Julia's calm reply proved she was no stranger to phone calls interrupting her life. "Tell her I'll meet her at Clearwater General. I'll be waiting when they pull in."

"I'll tell her." As the sound of the ambulance and a sheriff's cruiser drew closer, he leaned close, wanting the struggling woman to hear him. "She'll be at the hospital waiting for you. Hang on, okay?"

Tired green eyes stared up at him. "Do you think Miss Julia will take my baby?"

Tanner hesitated, confused. "You mean deliver the baby?"

Her bone-tired gaze said talking drained the last bit of energy she could muster. "I mean raise this baby. Care for her. Miss Julia's smart, and she'd be a good mother to this little girl. Before I go, I want to know my baby is taken care of. Loved. Miss Julia is the first person to treat me nice in a long time. I want her to have my baby."

Tanner kept a gentle grip on her hands and bent low. "I think you'd be a good mother to this little girl, too." He kept his voice soft and brushed back a lock of hair from her face. "She could be the best reason to change things up, Gracie."

"Gracie Jayne," she whispered, reminding him. "I won't be here to raise her, I know that. Miss Julia knows that. And I promised this baby I'd carry her as best I could, but I don't think we can go much farther."

Dire fear put a vise on Tanner's heart as the ambulance pulled into the lot behind him. "You hang on, let us get you to the hospital, and we'll see what's going on, okay? We'll let the doctors and Julia do their work. And no more talk of letting go, all right?"

The EMTs moved in, and her soft reply was whisked away by the sound of the gurney locks engaging and the gusting northwest wind.

And regardless of what he said, Tanner understood what he saw in Gracie Jayne's face. The pallor, the labored breathing, the struggle to speak a coherent thought. Had she walked from the bus stop three-quarters of a mile south of them again? In this wretched weather, in her condition?

First thing in the morning he was going to petition the City Transit Authority to reinstate the bus stop that used to be in the front loop of this broken-down parking lot. The stop had been discontinued a long time ago, but women using Julia's clinic shouldn't have to walk long blocks for help.

He waited while they secured Gracie Jayne in the ambulance, then followed them to the hospital. It seemed like hours away, although he knew better.

Would Julia be able to save Gracie Jayne? Would they be able to save the baby? And was Gracie Jayne serious about wanting Julia to take her child?

He pulled into the emergency room lot, parked and raced into the ER. Julia spotted him as he came through the door. She pointed up, which meant she wanted him to wait upstairs, in the OB unit, where expectant fathers and families shared joy and concern while babies made their final trek into the world.

Don't think about it. Just do it.

His conscience was right. This wasn't about him, it was about a woman's quest to bring her only child safely into the world, maybe before she left that same world.

Was God that harsh? Was he that cruel, that he'd separate mother and child at the juncture of birth and death?

You're blaming God again. Let's think twice before you go off the deep end, because Gracie

Jayne has been making rough choices for a very long time. How is that God's fault?

The common sense of the question broad-sided Tanner. Once he lost Ashley and Solomon, he'd been quick to blame God. But maybe free will and frailty of the human body should shoulder the majority of blame.

He paced in the small waiting area, wishing he could help. An elderly woman walked in and gave him a crooked smile tucked in a wealth of wrinkles. "Your first, I expect."

He shook his head. "Not mine, actually. A friend. But she's sick and it's not time for the baby yet."

"Oh, dear." She crossed the few feet separating them and grasped his hands. "Then we pray for God's will to be done!" With a surprisingly firm grip for someone her age, she started the Lord's Prayer. He stayed silent for the first few lines, but when she glared up at him as if he was some kind of heinous person for not joining in, he murmured the prayer along with her.

"It's always hardest at first," she told him as she plunked herself down into one of the corner chairs and pulled a knitting project out of her bag.

"Babies?" Tanner asked, but he half choked on the word because he knew that all too well.

"Praying." She jabbed a very sharp, pointed knitting needle his way and he decided not to be fooled by her diminutive size. "When you're out of practice, it seems awkward, but it gets better with time."

Could it? he wondered.

He'd prayed several times this evening, both on his own and under this little old woman's somewhat firm directive, and he hadn't been struck by lightning yet, which meant that maybe God wasn't the vindictive overlord he saw in his mind.

He sat across from her, watching as her aged fingers worked the combination of needles and rose-toned variegated yarn in lyrical motion. "You're expecting a girl?"

She glanced up, confused, then smiled at the incomplete project on her lap. "For a girl, yes."

"Is it your daughter? Or granddaughter?"

She shook her head. "Like you, I have no relative here."

"But—"

He wasn't sure he could figure this out, wasn't the least bit certain he even wanted to try, and when Julia walked in just then, he jumped up out of his seat. "How is she? How's Gracie Jayne?"

Her sad face told him what he didn't want

to hear, and his heart ground to a halt. "And the baby?"

"Holding her own and bigger than I thought."

"She'll be okay?"

"The neonatologists are with her now, but she's just over four-and-a-half pounds with good Apgar scores and a healthy set of lungs."

"Praise God!"

The old woman's words drew Julia's attention beyond Tanner. "Betsy, I didn't know you were here."

"I sensed trouble in the air," Betsy remarked, "and I came right over. I'm going to sit right here, quiet-like and knit and pray that baby to wellness."

"Thank you." Julia walked over to the elderly woman, leaned down and gave her a hug. "I'm grateful, as always."

Her words brought color to the old woman's cheeks. "Well, now. I do what I can, same as most."

"What happened, Julia?" Tanner took a step closer. "To Gracie Jayne?"

She hauled in a deep breath and stared beyond him for long moments, and when she finally turned his way, the pain in her gaze said she felt the loss of this woman deep into her soul. "Cancer. It was end-stage when she came to us a few weeks ago. I wanted to hospitalize her then, but she wouldn't hear of it. She had things to do. And so I let her go against my better judgment." Her sad expression said her worst fears had been realized. "And now she's gone."

"Could you have saved her? If she stayed in the hospital a few weeks ago?"

"No. But I could have made her more comfortable. And maybe have stretched things out another week or two for the baby's sake."

"Will the baby have cancer?"

She shook her head. "No. Treatment would have put the baby at risk, so Gracie Jayne wouldn't hear of it, but the baby should be fine." She hauled in another breath, one that sounded just as heartbroken as the first. "Our social worker is calling Human Services to let them know the baby's here."

"Why?"

"They'll need to place her when she's healthy enough."

He hesitated, unsure how to broach the subject and then waded in. "She wanted to know if you could raise the baby, Julia."

Julia paled. She stared at him as if she didn't trust her hearing. "What did you say?"

"When I was waiting for the ambulance with her, Gracie Jayne wanted to know if *you* would raise the baby. She said you were smart and you'd be a good mother to that little girl."

Quick tears slipped down Julia's cheeks, one after another. "Did she really say that?"

He nodded. "She said you'd been so kind to her and she knew you'd take good care of the baby."

"Not that it's any of my business," piped in Betsy from the corner, "but you've got room in that house, and plenty of family hereabouts. And a little girl would make a wonderful addition to your family, don't you think?"

Julia stared at her, then at Tanner. "I've just lost a patient and there's an orphaned baby fighting for her life in the NICU. Right now, I just want them to save that baby, and then we'll see what happens. With newborns so scarce for adoption, I expect there'll be a long line of approved applicants waiting for a phone call that a baby is available. It would be selfish of me to even think such a thing when I already have two kids. Wouldn't it?"

Tanner heard the words but didn't miss the note of hope in Julia's question.

"I shouldn't say more," Betsy remarked, her fingers marking stitch by stitch in quick, methodical fashion, "but folks 'round here know that Gracie Jayne Montgomery had a lot of problems in her day. Now maybe she cleaned them up and maybe she didn't, but it don't seem likely that folks waiting for a baby will take a chance on the premature daughter of a drug addict who died of cancer."

Julia's expression said that the truth of Betsy's words hit her hard. "You're right, of course. It's not always easy to place potentially sick or disabled children. And this baby might not have a thing wrong with her, but we can't predict that." She looked at Tanner again. "She really said that? And she managed to get to the clinic, trying to find me. Tanner, that's the greatest gift of all, the gift of a child."

He knew that. He'd had the unspeakable joy and unbearable sorrow merged into a day-long window. "It's something to think about, at least."

His words offered a sensible reprieve, but then Betsy made it even better by adding, "And pray. A child's worthy of every prayer we've got goin', to my way of thinkin'." Her tart voice said any fool should know that, and once again, Tanner couldn't disagree.

"You're both right." Julia turned toward Tanner. "Would you like to see her?"

The last time Tanner had walked into a NICU, he'd just said goodbye to his beloved wife, and twelve hours later had watched tiny Solomon breathe his last breath. He was on the verge of saying no, when Gracie Jayne's face came back to him…coming down the mountain, taking the bus, walking that last mile in wretched weather. She'd gone the distance at death's door. The least he could do was go welcome her baby daughter into the world. "Let's go."

Julia led the way through the double set of locked doors. They paused at the wide-basined sink and washed up, a procedure he remembered like it was yesterday. And by the time they got ready and were properly gowned, the nurse inside the NICU door buzzed them in.

A handful of babies were placed around the wide, deep room. In Erie, Solomon had been airlifted to a high-intensity NICU where the most fragile babies were taken. There had been over forty babies in that center, and the whole thing had seemed busy, volatile and crowded.

Here?

Monitors kept the staff aware of each baby's progress, but the setting was calmer. More sedate. "This is it?"

Julia turned, surprised. "As in…?"

"There's only a handful of babies here."

She nodded, still confused. "Well, we're a regional hospital, not a major city medical center. The critical babies get airlifted to Buffalo."

"Oh."

"You've been in a NICU before?" The question in her eyes urged him to spill the whole story, but then a tiny cry sounded to his right. He turned and saw Gracie Jayne's name on the card affixed to the head and foot of the crib. "This is her."

He stared down at the newborn girl, tiny by normal standards but robust compared to Solomon. He reached out a hand to touch her, then drew back. "Is it all right? Can I touch her?"

"Yes."

He barely waited for Julia's permission. It was as if his hand moved of its own accord, reaching across the heavy-gauge acrylic wall of the crib to touch the soft, thin skin of Gracie Jayne's daughter. He laid his finger against her hand, and when five tiny fingers closed around his pointer as if never intending to let go, those tiny fingers did the exact same thing to his heart.

He wasn't sure when he started crying. It didn't matter. Looking down, seeing this fragile baby girl staring up at him, clutching his hand, made him feel like now—*right now*—he could do anything and would do anything to make the world a better place for her.

"Amazing, right?" Julia whispered the words, shoved a clutch of tissues into his free hand and bumped shoulders with him. "You old softy. Who knew the big, brave and bold New York state trooper would get all mushy over an itty-bitty baby girl like this?"

"I blame her." Tanner tipped his gaze down. "She grabbed hold and who'd even think a newborn baby would do that? I think she likes me."

Julia smiled. "Well, who doesn't? Although you're a little moody for my tastes," she added, and he was instantly brought back to his almost taciturn afternoon behavior.

"I get stupid sometimes."

She shrugged. "We all do."

"Does that mean I'm forgiven?" He looked at her directly.

"Friends are allowed a bad day now and again."

The term *friends* meant he'd taken a firm step back. His fault, he knew, and his job was to make things right. "We need to talk soon. Have some time together and get to know each other."

Her yawn made him realize how late it had gotten, but then she smiled at the baby while keeping him at a polite but friendly distance. "Sure, we can talk. Sometime when I'm more awake."

"Are you going home now?"

"No can do. I've got a patient on the way in

for a labor check so I'll be here for the night most likely. Good night, baby girl." She stroked a finger along the curve of the baby's cheek. "God bless you."

"She doesn't have a name?"

"There wasn't time for names. We got her out alive. That was enough for the moment."

No name. No home. No one to love her, a perfectly beautiful baby girl, a child of the poor. "Is it all right if I come by to see her every day? So she has visitors?"

"I'll put your name on the list," Julia promised. She yawned, stretched and straightened. "I've got to finish up Gracie Jayne's chart and make sure everything's been organized for this baby. And listen, about Sunday? I haven't said anything to the boys about the monster truck show and it would probably be better if I go pick them up in Alfred on my own. Less confusing that way, and it won't mess up their bedtime."

He deserved the brush-off after ignoring her all afternoon, but that didn't make it easier to hear. "Let's not decide that now. Let's do it after we've both gotten some sleep."

Her hesitation said she'd prefer to have the matter settled, but she accepted his suggestion with a grimace as they walked out of the NICU together. "I'm not likely to change my mind."

"And I'm not likely to act like a jerk again, so maybe you will change your mind. Thank you." He raised his gaze to the double doors behind them. "For being here. Taking care of Gracie Jayne and that baby."

"It was a team effort, but you're welcome. Nobody in this business works alone."

Her words struck home as Tanner watched her stride back to the maternity hall. Medicine was a team effort, much like construction and police work. Everyone did their part for the best possible outcome. Did that happen behind the scenes at Ashley's obstetrical practice? Were they more of a team than he had believed?

They'd assured him that Ashley's heart condition had been undetectable, a fluke. In his anger and grief he chose not to believe them.

Marty's words came back to him. *It wasn't deliberate, they weren't trying to mess up my life...*

He slowed his steps toward the hospital exit. Maybe he was wrong to pursue the settlement. Perhaps he let the emotions of the moment and the groundswell of grief and anger push him to choices he wouldn't normally make. Was it too late to fix things?

His lawyer had taken this case with hearty enthusiasm. For Tanner to back out now would mean a hefty payment to the attorney out of his bank account, but at least he had a bank account.

Gracie Jayne's tattered image tweaked him. Upstairs, a nameless child struggled for life because her mother trusted Julia enough to make Herculean efforts. But not everything was in the midwife's hands. He saw that now.

Sleep was a long time in coming. Twice he heard a baby's cry, the phantom noise pulling him from restless slumber. When he finally did fall asleep, he managed to doze right through his alarm and if the neighbor's dog hadn't gone berserk chasing a squirrel, he'd have been late for work.

He swung by the hospital on his break, determined. He strode through the back entry, straight to the elevators, and took the quick ride up to the NICU. He spoke his name through the speaker. The nurse inside activated the door, which meant Julia remembered to put his name on the baby's visitation list. He set a box of candy on the counter of the nursing station, smiled, then crossed the short distance to the baby's crib.

She looked beautiful. Peaceful. Swaddled from neck to toe in a classic hospital blanket, she was sound asleep. The nurse came over, checked the monitors, then nodded, satisfied. "She's doing great. Are you the father?"

"Just a friend."

That term made the nurse smile. "Can't have too many of those. She was a little restless at first, but getting born takes a lot out of you. Now?" She indicated the monitors alongside the crib. "She's been solid for over eight hours, which means she's adjusting well. Let me know if you need anything, okay?"

"Okay."

"Tanner?"

He spotted Julia, then tapped his watch. "Shouldn't you be sleeping?"

"I'm heading home now, but I wanted to check in on her. How's she doing?"

"Solid, according to the nurse. And beautiful."

"She is a pretty little thing." Julia smiled down at the precious infant, and the sight of her, bending over this orphaned child, was a sight Tanner could get used to seeing every day.

A sudden break in the thick, March cloud cover brought sunlight streaming into the nursery from the bank of south-facing windows. "Oh, it's good to see the sun," Julia whispered. "It's been a long, cold winter. I'm ready for spring."

"Me, too." He smiled at her, and when she aimed a tired smile back his way, his heart opened wider, at long last. Was it the warmth of the sun flooding the tiles above the baby's crib? Or the warmth in Julia's eyes as she watched over someone else's child? Or maybe it was simply his heart breaking free at last, shrugging off the layers of grief and anger that shackled him for so long.

He didn't know and he really didn't care, because he hadn't seen the glass half-full in a long time. Now hope had taken root within him and he was determined to somehow, some way, make it flourish.

Chapter Ten

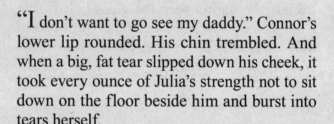

"I don't want to go see my daddy." Connor's lower lip rounded. His chin trembled. And when a big, fat tear slipped down his cheek, it took every ounce of Julia's strength not to sit down on the floor beside him and burst into tears herself.

"Will he remember us?" Martin's cautious voice held a hidden question. After over two years of no personal contact, he was probably wondering if he'd remember his father, an understandable question from a seven-year-old.

"Yes." Julia didn't elaborate. Vic wasn't evil, the boys would be in no danger, but they deserved more than his casual interest now and again. That was out of her hands, though, and maybe they'd come back on Sunday rested, refreshed and with a renewed relationship with their father.

And maybe pigs will fly.

She shut down her cynical inner voice, helped the boys stow their backpacks into the back of her SUV and drove up the road to pick Piper up. Her sister-in-law hurried out, climbed into the front seat, high-fived the boys, then faced Julia. "I owe you. Big-time."

Julia put the car into gear and frowned. "For what?"

"Rescuing me. I love my husband, but the thought of getting out of the house for a few hours, traveling with my peeps—" she aimed a broad smile at the boys in the backseat, then slipped each of them a homemade chocolate chip cookie "—and road food has made my day."

"Zach getting restless?"

"Your brother was born restless," Piper retorted. "So this immobility is killing him, and he goes from being wonderful to crabby at warp speed. Then the cycle starts all over again."

"Pain meds aren't helping?"

"He's weaned himself off of them, a gesture I respect from a distance. Up close?" She gave an over-exaggerated sigh for everyone's benefit. "Not so much. They told us it would be a twelve-week recovery, so we need to be patient.

Both of us," she added and nipped a cookie for herself. "Jules, do you want a cookie?"

"Nope." Nerves were gnawing on her stomach, and she'd made it through nearly three weeks of choosing her foods with more care. Five pounds had disappeared with little trouble or thought on her part. "I'm saving my calories for Easter."

"Smart move." Piper turned back toward the boys. "I brought puzzle books for you guys." She handed them over the seat, then offered each boy a pencil. "I had to hunt to find these. We used to love to do these on car trips when we were little."

"You didn't wanna just watch a movie?" Connor asked.

"Listen, kid, there were no TVs in cars in my day. Let's see how many puzzles you guys can get done in the next half hour. Ready? Set. Go!" She smiled when the boys bent over their respective puzzle books.

Julia shot her a quiet look of gratitude. Anything that kept the boys occupied for the next hour would be welcome, and if it helped alleviate their worries about spending time with their absentee father, that would be all the better. Julia's phone buzzed with a text a few minutes later. "Piper, can you check that for me, please?"

Piper nodded, picked up the phone, then smiled. "Thinking of you. Praying. Tanner."

A surge of delight flowed through her that Tanner was thinking of her. Praying for her. He seemed to know how hard this whole weekend was going to be.

But she'd put an intentional lock on her heart after his unpredictable actions yesterday. Never again would she put herself in the position of having to prove herself to a man. Or to anyone, for that matter. She deserved to be loved and cherished just as she was, and Tanner's reticence raised warning flags.

She'd back away quietly, despite how she felt whenever he walked into a room. She'd give him polite smiles, when what she really wanted to do was laugh with him. Joke with him. Spar with him.

Being around Tanner made her feel vulnerable and that brought up feelings of inadequacy. She hadn't been able to make Vic happy. She'd pulled out all the stops and it still wasn't enough. She'd learned a hard lesson, but she learned it well and she'd never put herself in that situation again.

She turned onto the Alfred/Almond exit ramp and grappled her emotions. She wouldn't cry, even though every part of her wanted to turn the car around and head back to Kirkwood as fast as she could. She fought the dread in her chest and pulled into the almost empty convenience store parking lot.

She glanced around.

No Vic.

She was a few minutes early, so she moved across the street, got the boys out of the car and let them run around on the nearby playground. Minutes ticked by. Ten. Then fifteen. She was on the verge of calling Vic because he was nearly a half hour late, when a sleek black muscle car cruised into the convenience store lot. It pulled to a stop and Vic climbed out one side.

And a skinny, young, long-legged brunette climbed out the other.

Suddenly five pounds wasn't enough. Because to compete with this young woman Julia would have to erase a dozen years and twenty pounds and stretch marks and—

"Stop it right now," Piper warned. "He's doing what Zach said he always does. All show, no substance."

Julia breathed deep, nodded to Piper and pasted a smile on her face before she called his name. "We're over here."

Vic turned, realized he had to either bring the boys' things across the road or drive over to the playground, and he stopped, no doubt waiting for her to grab the boys and run them across the street to the appointed meeting place.

Not gonna happen, buddy.

Annoyed, he climbed back into the showy car, waited while his companion did the same, then spun gravel as he made the turn onto the two-lane. He pulled into the playground parking lot a few hundred feet down the road and the car ground to a quick stop.

He climbed out again, but having to do it twice ruined the effect, and Julia had to swallow a laugh. He'd planned his late entrance to show her what she was missing—and what he preferred—but he hadn't expected her to take control of the situation, which made it that much sweeter.

But then Connor started to cry.

Martin hung back, unsure.

And when Vic stepped forward, Martin climbed right back into the car, into his seat, fastened his belt and hit the locks.

He might be quiet, he might be a little shy, but Martin had made himself clear: he wanted nothing to do with his father, the beefed-up car or the leggy brunette with great hair.

"I don't have time for this." Vic glowered

at Julia. She felt Piper come up alongside, and held her off with a hand of caution.

"Hi, Vic. Nice to see you, too. How've you been?"

"Don't start with me, Julia. I need to get back on the road because at the end of today's drive, I've got to get two kids to bed."

"Go talk to them. And be nice. They're amazingly wonderful little boys, but you've lost ground the past two years. Relationships don't get fixed overnight."

He stared at her. "If you hadn't moved three hours away, we wouldn't be having this problem."

If you'd remained faithful to the vows you spoke on our wedding day, we wouldn't be having this problem...

She kept silent and crouched next to Connor. "Connor, this is your father."

"I don't think I like him." The boy meant no disrespect, but the honesty of youth took precedence. "Is he mean, Mommy?"

"No, I'm not mean, but I do mean what I say." Vic came down to Connor's level, too, but it was clear he didn't like the gesture. "I teach kids in school every day, and they would say I'm strict but I'm fair."

"I don't know what that means." Connor

whispered the words into Julia's ear as he shrunk closer to her side. "Does he like us?"

"I love you."

Connor looked unconvinced. Martin stayed locked in the car, arms folded, refusing to look at his father.

"Julia, unlock the door and get Martin out. We need to be on our way."

She started to answer him, but then the brunette moved to Martin's side of the car and said, "Martin, I'm Cassidy and I've got a little brother just about your age. I'm going to take a little time to swing on the swings, and I bet your dad will join me. Come on over, sit and chat, and maybe we can talk about the next superhero movie that's coming out."

She waited by the car for just a moment, then started to ease away, allowing Martin time to answer. The young woman—Cassidy—showed more finesse at dealing with kids than Vic ever had.

"You like them?" Martin asked through the narrow window opening.

She swung back and smiled. "Love them is more like it. *Iron Man* is my brother's favorite, but I'm a *Wolverine* gal myself." She paused, giving him time to think, and Julia appreciated the young woman's kind efforts to defuse the situation. "Do you have a favorite?"

He stuttered then, an old problem that hadn't reared its head in nearly three years. *"C-C-Captain America."*

"He's amazing," she agreed, then went to sit on the swings.

Vic grumbled something under his breath, shot a dark look at Julia, then took another swing. Julia grasped Connor's little hand, sat at the edge of the nearby picnic table and faced the younger woman. "I'm Julia Harrison, Vic's ex-wife. This is Connor."

Connor nestled in a little closer to her side.

"And that's Martin in the car. And this is my sister-in-law, Piper Harrison."

"Zach got married." Vic's flat tone implied that Zach's marital status bored him.

"I was a ring bearer in Uncle Zach's wedding," Connor whispered. He peeked up at Cassidy. "I got to ride in a limo and wave out the top and drink bubbly stuff. And I danced with my mom. A lot."

"Oh, that sounds fun." Cassidy smiled at him and Connor loosened his grip on Julia's shirt. "I was in my sister's wedding last year and I had a nice time, too. Was your brother in the wedding?"

"He was the head ring bearer," Connor explained with all the seriousness a five-year-old could muster. "I was still little and Martin knew 'zactly what to do."

"I bet he did." Cassidy sent a smile toward Martin, but didn't rush the situation, even though Vic's body language said he was chomping at the bit. "Are you in school, Connor?"

"I'm in kindergarten and Miss Dubois is my teacher and she says I'm very smart and I try to be smarter than everyone else, every day, and I don't beat anyone up."

"Perfect." Cassidy smiled down at him, and held up her hand for a high five that Connor met with gusto. "That's the best of both worlds right there. Smart and nice."

"Your lawyer contacted me."

Julia shifted her attention to Vic. "A matter we can discuss in private. Away from little ears."

"Or not worth discussing at all." Vic's eyes sharpened. "You took the children to the other side of the state, then expected me to hand over a substantial portion of my pay for their care. That's unsustainable, of course."

"Not a topic that's open for conversation right now," she replied, and then she stood. "Have your people talk to my people. As I said, it's not a subject we should be discussing here." She sent Connor a deliberate look, then called Martin's name.

He stared at her from the backseat of the car, then sighed, and if she allowed herself to get caught up in that sigh, she'd take the boys home and never turn back. But that wouldn't be fair, and she'd promised herself and God that she'd be as fair as she could be.

Which meant Martin had to give this a try. "Martin, I've got to head back to Kirkwood. Aunt Piper has things to do and I've got to check in at the hospital." She wasn't scheduled to check in, but she would stop by and peek in on Gracie Jayne's baby. She'd sat and rocked the tiny girl twice that day. No family had stepped forth as yet, and for the moment, the newborn was a lost lamb in need of love. "Come on, honey. Come say hi to your dad and shake his hand. You know what Grandpa always says, that we've got to give things a chance."

Martin held her gaze through the window, finally sighed and undid his seat belt. He unlocked the door, then climbed out of the backseat. "I don't think Grandpa was talking about this." He stared at his father, and suddenly meek, mild Martin looked far more like his namesake grandfather than he had in the past.

"I think Grandpa means we have to try our best, all the time, like he does."

"Mr. Perfect." Vic muttered the words just loud enough for Julia to hear them. To Martin, he said, "And that's sound advice. If you don't give me a chance to be a good father, how can we know? And do you remember when you were little how much you used to like following me around? Pretending to be big like me?"

"I remember." His tone said he didn't recall the moments with the same level of enthusiasm. He turned toward his mother. "We have to go?"

She didn't want to nod, but she did. "Yes. And I'll be here on Sunday at three to pick you up." Remembering how late Vic was today, she pulled an ace out of her bag and prayed Tanner hadn't given away the tickets he'd purchased. "We're taking the boys to the monster truck show on Sunday afternoon, so they can't get here late."

"The monster truck show?" Martin's eyes grew round. "There's a bunch of kids from my class going to the monster truck show! I never thought we'd be able to go, Mom!" He grabbed her around the waist and hugged her tight. "We'll be here right on time, I promise. And we might be able to get the Extreme Dominator's picture!"

"I bet we can." She bent down and hugged him while Piper withdrew their backpacks from the SUV. "And, boys, you can call me anytime. Your father has a phone and you know my number, so if you want to talk to me, just call."

"We will."

"Okay."

She couldn't stay properly calm at this final parting moment. She kissed both their cheeks, offered a cheery wave and climbed into the car quickly. Piper hopped into the passenger seat and turned her head away while Julia steered the car up onto the road, then hooked a left onto the I-86 entrance ramp. Even tough-as-nails Piper was having a hard time leaving the boys behind.

Julia wanted to stomp on the brakes, go back and save her boys from the clutches of their foolish, narcissistic father. For just a moment she understood the desperation of people who flee with their children, but common sense scoffed at the emotion.

Vic was their father. If his resolve to redevelop a relationship with his sons fizzled, at least she wouldn't be held responsible.

Tears flowed, and she knew it was insensible. He was their father.

But his cool rebuffs, barely restrained frustration and his negativity…those factors stirred up emotions better left buried.

Her phone rang just then. Tanner's number showed up in the dashboard display. She swiped away the tears and hit the button. "Hey."

"Hey, yourself. You okay? Because you don't sound okay."

"No." She couldn't lie to him. Not when the concern in his voice said he genuinely cared. "But I'll be okay. Vic was late so we just got on the road. Piper's pretending not to cry."

"I am not," Piper sniped from the seat next to her, then gave a short and unhappy sigh. "I'm fully admitting that I wanted to grab those boys, put them in the car and run for the hills. Tears are understandable."

"I hear you. This is a tough and huge first step," Tanner acknowledged. It was a new beginning…and Julia had aced them before. She could do it again now. "I wanted to check in, let you know I was thinking about you, Julia."

Thinking about her. Calling to see if she was all right. Respecting her. The simple beauty of that lessened the weight on her heart. "Thank you, Tanner."

"What are you doing tonight?"

Piper poked her, but the last thing Julia

wanted to do was pretend to have fun. "Getting some things done at home."

"Well, that's a horrible idea when I've got the night off. I'm going to visit the baby, then grab supper. Eating with me is a much better idea."

She didn't need Piper's second poke to realize he was right. "When are you going to see the baby?"

"About the same time you are, I expect."

She laughed, because even in the short time they'd known each other, he realized how important children were in her life. Her boys, delivering babies, Gracie Jayne's tiny blessing. "I hate that she doesn't have a name."

"Me, too." He paused for a moment. "So I gave her a nickname. I call her 'princess,' and she kind of smiles when I say it."

Julia's heart tipped more firmly in his direction. "I love it, Tanner. It's perfect." She drew a breath, tried not to think about what she'd just left behind and said, "I think visiting Princess together sounds wonderful."

"It's a plan. I'll see you in about ninety minutes."

"Okay."

She hung up the phone and glanced sideways at Piper. "Hush."

"I'm not saying a word," Piper replied, but

her smug face said plenty. "But I woulda smacked you if you said no. Nicely, of course."

Julia had never had a sister, but now that she'd kind of inherited Piper and her sister, Rainey, as family? She was really glad to be surrounded by God-loving, stand-your-ground women. With Vic's sudden reentrance into their lives, she was pretty sure she'd need the women's support and wasn't afraid to ask for it.

Chapter Eleven

Tanner had one goal for the evening, and that was to keep Julia from worrying nonstop. She spotted him as he crossed the hospital parking lot, and her joyful expression said she was just as glad to see him. He reached out, pulled her into a hug they both needed and held on.

Holding Julia felt right.

The scent of her hair, softly curling beneath his chin, the feel of her breathing, a little catch now and then, but then she leaned back, looked up and he had no other choice but to kiss her.

Perfect.

The single word described the emotions grabbing him at that moment.

He could get used to this. He had a lot to tell her, a lot to share, to confess, but kissing Julia took precedence right now.

She pulled back and glanced around, cha-grined. "We're kissing in a public place."

"We should stop that this instant." He gave her a gentle kiss on the cheek and made it a point to take his time. "Except stopping is the last thing on my mind, but Princess is expecting us. Let's go." He took her hand, and when they got inside, he didn't let go and she didn't pull away, which made the moment even more wonderful.

They took the elevator to the NICU area, and she clung to his hand the way he held hers, as if holding hands meant something dear and precious.

"Hey, Princess." Julia stroked one finger along the baby's cheek and lifted her up. "Wanna rock her?"

"Yes." He sat down, smiled up at Julia and accepted the baby. She stirred, squeaked and stretched, then buttoned her eyes closed in continued slumber. "She's amazing, Julia."

"And you're adorable with her," Julia teased. She took out her cell phone and snapped a pic of him, then showed him the image a few seconds later. "The big bad cop and the innocent baby. That's a wall portrait right there."

It felt weird to see an image of himself holding a baby, as if he was somehow being unfair to Solomon's memory.

And yet, if things had gone well back then, he and Ashley would have most likely welcomed a second baby by now. The human heart's capacity to love knew no bounds. Right now, holding this gift that came from God and Gracie Jayne's diligence, he felt like he was doing the right thing. "Still no news on family?"

Julia pulled a second rocking chair up alongside him. "The social worker has found some family. No one is interested in this baby at this point. There are legal issues to be dealt with, and there is a foster family willing to take her in Depew—"

"Why so far?" Tanner interrupted. "There's no one in this area who can take her?" The idea that no one in their county wanted Princess appalled him. What was the matter with people?

She reached a hand up to his cheek. "Because there were no legally drawn-up papers, Princess becomes a ward of the court. They get to decide where she goes, and a premature baby who might or might not have special needs can't go to just any home. Those homes have to be certified to meet unexpected needs or situations."

"And there are none of those here?" He

didn't bother to hide his disbelief. "That can't be right."

"There are some, but they've already got babies," she explained. "So Princess—"

"Gets shipped off an hour north and makes it a lot harder for us to drop in and see her."

"It looks that way."

The baby squirmed again. She gave out a plaintive cry and Julia retrieved a bottle from the nurse. She handed Tanner the bottle and he stared at it. "I'm going to feed her?"

"She's hungry and you're holding her. Do the math."

He gulped, repositioned the baby and put the bottle near her mouth. She groped for it instantly, found the nipple and began sucking with gusto, hands fisted. "She's very intense." He turned his attention to Julia. "Is that normal?"

"Instinctive and normal and good to see," Julia told him. "They said she was being a lazy eater the first day and that concerned them, but there's nothing laid-back about the way she's attacking that bottle."

"You can say that again." He smiled down at the baby, then leaned down and kissed her soft forehead. "She's got a trucker's appetite today." He sat back and savored the moment while cautioning himself. He had no ties to this child, no say in her future. To let himself love her was a mistake, but as he wiped a tiny drop of milk from her cheek, reality hit.

Too late.

He'd fallen hard for both the baby and her not-so-legal guardian. The question now was what to do about it. Marty had given him fair warning. As a cop, he knew better than to get himself into an uncontrollable situation, and yet here he was, ready to run the risk of loving again.

"Almost three ounces." The baby's nurse smiled at them as she noted the feeding on Princess's chart. "That's her best one yet. You folks are good for her."

Those simple words meant so much to Tanner. As he handed the baby to the nurse, a flash of insight drew him upright. For three years he'd carried failure on his back, bearing responsibility for Ashley's and Solomon's deaths. On top of that, he was suing the medical team because someone had to be at fault. If only he'd pushed Ashley to a different doctor, a different practice, if only he'd—

Reality broadsided him. Ashley knew her own mind, she knew what she wanted and she was a smart, educated woman. If she felt safe with her choices, who was he to second-guess her? Maybe the folks around him were right, maybe things just happened sometimes, and maybe…

It wasn't God's or anyone's fault, it was just life.

Julia kissed the baby's forehead. "Good night, sweet pea. See you tomorrow." She faced the nurse and pointed toward the social worker's office around the corner. "Nothing from Wanda today?"

"Not a peep. And this baby's got a little time with us," the NICU nurse said, smiling down at the now-sleeping Princess, "because she needs to put on some weight, but she's doing great now. No problems that we see. Holding her own completely."

"That's good to hear." Tanner stroked the baby's head and met Julia's gaze, and for that moment, the world became a more perfect place. Him. Julia. This baby. Right then it looked entirely possible, although several factors stood in the way. The words of a childhood pastor came back to him and he whispered them as he said goodbye to the baby. "With God, all things are possible."

Julia looked up at him. "I don't generally hear you quoting scripture, Tanner. And the look in your eyes says you're making plans."

"I'm a planner by nature." He settled his gaze on her, kissed the baby and then slung an arm around Julia's shoulders as they moved to the door. "I'd forgotten that for a while, but something about being here with you and her has rejuvenated that instinct."

"It's hard to walk away, though."

The catch in Julia's voice said she meant more than the baby. He gripped her shoulder and pulled her a little closer. "But she's in good hands. And we'll be back tomorrow. And Sunday's not that far away."

He expected her to cry.

She didn't. She breathed deeply, reached up and touched his cheek briefly, but the quick caress created a kinship of hope. He leaned down, planted a lazy kiss to her hair, then pulled open the exit door for her. "Let's eat, and you can fill me in on what still needs to be done with the clinic. The next time someone comes out of the hills looking for help, I want it to be right there, no sideways trips to the main office."

"You mean that?" She stopped and faced him. "Even though we might be a magnet for trouble?"

"Magnets lose their draw after a while, and it will be our job to make that happen," he promised. "If we discourage the bad guys from hanging around, they'll find another place."

"As long as the women are safe." She ig-

nored the cold west wind and looked up, cha-
grined. "We considered proximity when we
picked that spot, but we never thought that
thugs might put the women in danger. With
the brick through the front window, it's become a concern."

"It's cold, about to rain again and I'm hungry. I'll meet you over at The Pelican's Nest,
okay? We'll carry on our discussion over hot
food and Tina's desserts, a guy and his girl,
out having a late Friday night dinner."

"I'm not your girl."

He grazed one thumb across the base of her
chin. Held her gaze. "Give me a little time,
Julia. Give me time."

Her heart tripped faster. Harder.

Julia wanted to grab hold of him and never
let go, but was that because of the emotions
of the moment or the pain of leaving the boys
with their father for the weekend?

She wasn't sure, and she wanted to be absolutely, positively, 100 percent certain. *I don't
think it works that way*, her conscience advised.
There's always chance involved. That's life.

Julia had taken her share of chances. Em-
bracing another one now seemed both tempt-
ing and wrong. But she realized, she had to
start trusting herself again. Trusting God. Life

was a gift. It was about time she started living the gift again.

"Julia!" Tina waved from the other side of the restaurant counter a few minutes later. "How'd today go, honey? And what are you doing here this late? I— Oh." She stopped talking as Tanner walked through the door. "Table for two?"

"Perfect," said Tanner. Julia had the urge to administer a wake-up call with her heel to his instep, because if he treated this like a date, then the entire town would see it that way. Currently there were only three other tables being used, but in a small town, everyone would know by tomorrow. "Tina, do you still have fish available?"

"Best haddock in Western New York," she promised. "And coffee? Or is it too late for coffee?"

"Water's good for me," Julia answered. She slid into a booth overlooking the dark, gray, windswept lake, then turned her back on purpose. Slate-gray waves held little comfort, and soon she'd be going home to a mostly empty house. At least her dad would be there, milling about in the morning, back and forth to the farm, restlessly awaiting spring's softer weather. Maybe that tree falling on her house did her a favor because she wouldn't have to be alone this weekend or spring break week.

"I was thinking we should give the entry to the clinic a brighter tone."

"What?"

"The entry to the clinic," Tanner said. "Can we make it brighter? More inviting?"

"We could, but that's not my forte," Julia confessed. "I'm out of my element when it comes to that kind of thing."

"What about yellow?' he asked. "Neutral, but bright and inviting."

"With floral prints from the ones Mrs. Thurgood left me." Tina deposited waters on the table and pulled up a chair. "She was such a sweet soul, and she loved helping people. She'd have been the first person to jump on board and help you with your project, Julia." She took a seat at the end of their table. "I don't mean to interrupt your date, but—"

"It's not a date," Julia assured her.

Tanner's lazy smile said the exact opposite.

Tina ignored Julia's protest and leaned forward. "I think Tanner's got a great idea, and what a nice tribute it would be to Mrs. Thurgood to have some of her paintings on the wall."

"They'd be beautiful," Julia agreed. "You don't mind donating them?"

"She left me a dozen and that's about eight too many," Tina replied. "So that will liven things up nicely over there. Two fish fries?"

Tanner quickly nodded yes.

Julia hesitated. She knew she should have hers broiled, no butter. And a side salad, no croutons. And lemon water. She was about to say exactly that, when she caught Tanner's eye, and realized she was allowing self-doubt to dictate too much of her life. Her food, her clothes, her shoes… "I'd love a fish fry, and extra tartar sauce please. But instead of French fries, can I have a double coleslaw, Tina? And how is Charley doing? I haven't seen her in weeks and at this stage, they grow so quickly."

"Charley's gorgeous, and she has Max wrapped around her pretty little finger. I can't believe that not so long ago I was single, grumpy and lost my business to arson, and now?" She flicked a glance around. "This. Married, a baby, a cute house on the hill and a family business. I was ready to hit the road, get away from Kirkwood and never look back."

"But you didn't."

"I couldn't leave Max's parents in a lurch, not with his father so sick. And I didn't really want to leave. I love Kirkwood, but I wanted everything to be all right. On my terms. And my timeline."

"And God doesn't always work that way." Julia knew that firsthand.

"A fact I discovered." Tina winked at them before she moved back to the kitchen area. "I'll let you guys resume your conversation."

Julia turned. Caught Tanner's eyes. And for the life of her she couldn't recall what they'd been discussing two minutes before.

He grinned. "Yellow paint."

She breezed on as if she'd known that all along. "And we've got a bunch of folding chairs donated from the women's shelter in Clearwater. And Jenny Campbell found us two end tables for the waiting area, and wondered if she should paint them, so I'll tell her yes. If we pick out the yellow paint at Campbell's Hardware, then Jenny can pick a paint that complements the walls."

"And washable floors."

"With nonskid entry rugs because we get six months of rain and snow, sleet and ice," she agreed. "I think we're on track to open as scheduled, and what a perfect way to finish the Lenten season. Prayer, sacrifice and a new clinic for women in need. The church is sponsoring an Easter egg hunt on Holy Saturday. Rainey, Tina and Laura are organizing it. I promised the boys I'd take them."

"I've never been to one," Tanner admitted.

"Never?" The thought of never going to an Easter egg hunt seemed almost impossible. "Not even when you were a kid?"

He shrugged. "We went to a couple of different churches. Never stayed long at any particular one. My parents spent most of their time fighting. Nothing was easy when they got divorced, so the normal kid things got pushed aside."

Two things instantly went through Julia's mind. One, that Tanner's description sounded like a wretched way to grow up, to be caught between warring parents all the time. Where was the love in that scenario?

And the second thought?

She was going to make sure she didn't make the same mistake with Martin and Connor. If Vic intended to be part of their lives, she needed to let him, and without the resentment she'd embraced since his initial phone call. Putting the boys first should take precedence. She needed to remind herself of that more often. "Well, then I'd like to invite you to the egg hunt. I'm on call that night, but the boys and I are going, and it would be great if you could go, too."

His face shadowed slightly, but then he reached out, gripped her hand and nodded. "I'd like that. I'm working that evening, too, but I'm free in the morning and I can't think of anything I'd like better. Unless it's a monster truck show at the arena this Sunday."

She laughed. "Yes, you were right to hang on to the tickets. The boys are so excited about going."

"Well, the Extreme Dominator and the Crusher are scheduling a grudge match. And there'll be cotton candy. What more could a boy want?"

Tina brought their food then, and sitting there, talking with Tanner, eating some of the best fried fish known to man, made the weekend seem less troubling.

"How's your fish?"

"The best I've ever had," she told him, laughing. "I'm so glad I didn't wimp out and get the broiled fish. This is amazing. Thank you, Tanner."

"You're welcome."

Just then, his phone buzzed. Julia glanced down. "Do you need to take that?"

He frowned as he read the text. Concern darkened his face, and then he set the phone back down. "Nothing that can't wait."

His expression said the message bothered him. Julia had the urge to reach out. Smooth his troubled brow. Let him lean into her strength, making both of them stronger.

Silly, of course. What would a man like Tanner need support for? He was big, strong and rugged. And yet, every now and again, she sensed an emptiness in him. She recognized it because she'd felt that way several times over the past few years. She'd lost her unborn daughter, then her mother, followed by her father's wretched diagnosis with Alzheimer's and Vic's affairs with younger women. The multiple crises had tested her faith and endurance, but with each sorrow she'd clung to motherhood as her mainstay. Putting the boys first meant she couldn't wallow in pain or sadness. Her strategy worked. Faith, motherhood and keeping busy kept her focused on tomorrow as she struggled to put the roughed-up yesterdays in perspective.

She glanced at her watch. "We've got to go. They'll want to close up here, and I'm at the hospital early in the morning. And then I'm going to see if they've made any progress at all on my poor house..."

"The weather's made rebuilding that back wall a challenge, hasn't it?"

"That's for certain. It's time for winter to end and spring to take hold," she said. She reached for her jacket, but he was too quick. He held it open, and stepping into the sheepskin coat felt like stepping into his arms. Warm.

Inviting. Cozy. "I know it's only mid-March, but I'm so done with winter."

He gave her shoulders a gentle squeeze of agreement. "A little madness in the spring is welcome even for the king."

"You quote Dickinson?" Julia squinted her eyes at him. "Poetry lover, lawman and all-around nice guy?"

"Yes to the latter two. And I was required to have four credits of English at Fredonia. Poetry looked easy. It wasn't, by the way."

She laughed, waved good-night to Tina and preceded him out the door. "I love poetry, but it's rare to find a guy who can quote something older than lines from *Star Wars*."

Tanner grasped her hands as they reached her car. He lifted them to his mouth, kissed them, then opened her car door and probably had no clue how the gallant gesture affected her. Rain? What rain?

"Get in. You're getting soaked."

Right then, she didn't care. At this moment, the rain and wind meant nothing, but she climbed in and opened the window as an invitation.

Tanner didn't need to be asked twice. He leaned in, ignoring the rain pelting his back and lingered over the kiss good-night.

Her breath caught. Her heart stammered

because she knew, oh, she knew right then, that this man had captured her heart.

It felt marvelous to throw caution to the winds and fall in love with Tanner. Right now, she didn't want to ponder what-ifs. She'd have plenty of time to reflect on that later, but now she let herself get trapped in the romance of the moment, the wind, the rain, the warmth, the kiss…

"Julia." He whispered her name and set his forehead against hers, his breathing ragged.

"I know."

He smiled. She felt the curve of his lips and the rise of his cheeks in the darkness and then he planted one last kiss on her mouth before easing out of the car window. "I'm soaked."

She nodded. "It's your giving nature. I love that about you, Tanner."

His grin widened. "Good to know. I'll stop in to see the little princess tomorrow."

"I'm at the hospital until three."

"If you're busy when I get there, I'll leave a note."

She laughed and waved to him as he climbed into his car.

A note. Cute. Fun. Romantic. No one did that kind of thing anymore, did they?

The old-fashioned idea left her anticipating the chance of getting a note from Tanner.

When she got home, her father and Laura were sitting on the couch watching one of the last preseason baseball games. "Didn't I just leave you at the restaurant?" Julia asked as she hung up her wet jacket by the fire.

"I ducked out when you guys were half-done," Laura replied. "Tina's closing up. Marty said there was a fire, baseball and popcorn over here. What woman can resist an offer like that?"

Marty's smile said it had worked.

"Who's winning?"

Two guilty looks said they hadn't been paying much attention to the game. "Well, I'm on call first thing, so I'm going to bed. Good night, guys."

"Good night, honey."

"'Night, Julia."

She climbed the short staircase to her room. Ice-cold rain and wind scrubbed the west-facing windows but the shared look from her father to Laura D'Allesandro downstairs said regardless of the cold, wet weather, spring was definitely in the air.

Chapter Twelve

Tanner read the text from his attorney one more time.

The court had set a preliminary hearing date for the following Friday. In six short days, he could be face-to-face with the medical professionals in charge of Ashley's prenatal treatment. He'd waited for this day for over two years.

Now?

Dread filled him like a slow-moving storm front. What had felt right in the depths of his loss and anger, seemed cold and unconscionable now that he knew Julia, saw her work, her goals, her heart and, yes, her soul.

You wanted to blame someone. Somebody had to be at fault. Maybe you've learned that's not always the case?

He had, but what to do about it? He walked

through the dark condo once again, surveying the storm beyond the insulated glass, but not really seeing it.

He texted the lawyer back. We need to talk ASAP.

He didn't expect a reply tonight, but he got one. Call tomorrow @ 1.

He'd call him off, Tanner decided, and when he made that decision, a thousand-pound weight slid off his shoulders. Weeks earlier he'd been vested in this course of action, but everything had changed since meeting Julia.

And falling in love with her.

He needed to end the lawsuit and move on with his life. Was it chance that put him on that snowy overpass the night Julia decided to check out the new clinic with her flashlight?

No. God, he decided. And while he wasn't too up on the whole faith thing, his life had been changed that evening. Seeing her. Realizing that he was being thrust into situations to shake him out of his doldrums.

It had worked. Somewhere in the ensuing weeks, he'd begun to live again. Love again. Laugh again. And he wanted to do more of that with Julia and those boys.

His phone rang, unusual for a Friday night. Neda's name showed up in the bar and he answered the call quickly. "Hey, sis. What's up? Everything okay?"

She hesitated and he sensed her surprise. "I didn't expect you to answer because you never do, which makes me wonder what's going on? Are you okay?"

"I am. Yes. Finally."

"Really, Tanner? Because I've been worried about you for so long that it's going to be really hard for me to stop, but I'm willing to do it! Just say the word."

"I'm better. Much better. And you shouldn't be wasting your time worrying about me when you've got a beautiful family there to take up your time."

"*You're* my family, too," she insisted. The warmth of her voice reminded him of growing up side by side, dealing with their parents. They'd done all right eventually, but he saw the residual scarring more clearly now. He'd been in danger of becoming harsh and embittered, like his parents, but Neda had persisted to love him. Stay in contact. Even when he wouldn't answer her calls. "And I'll spend my time as I see fit, big brother. Praying for you wasn't a hardship. It was an honor. But I'm so glad to hear you sounding like the old Tanner. I love you."

"I love you, too," he told her. He wished he

could take back the past years of shying away from her kids, their birthdays, their family celebrations. Shame on him for being that guy. From this moment on, he was determined to handle whatever God sent his way. "Are you doing anything special for Easter?"

"We're going to Jeremy's parents' after Good Friday services here. You should join us. There's plenty of room, plenty of food and the kids would love to see you."

He'd like to see them, too, but Julia would be sending her boys back to Ithaca the day after Easter, which meant he'd really like to share the day with them. "How about if I come down for a day during spring break? Are you guys going away?"

"We're staying right here, so that would be wonderful. I'll cook all your favorite foods."

"Steak on the grill and bakery rolls. Perfect."

She laughed. "Works for me! The kids made Easter cards for you. We mailed them today, so watch for them, okay?"

"I will. And, Neda? Thanks for calling. I love you."

"Me, too. Talk to you soon."

He hung up the phone, glad he'd answered it. He slept that night, the whole night, and woke up in the morning feeling good. Strong. Invigorated.

He stopped by the hospital just before noon. The duty nurse smiled when she saw him. "Perfect timing. Julia was here earlier but our little princess was a sleepyhead. Now she's awake and fairly sure we're starving her. Would you like to feed her?"

"Absolutely." He settled into the oak rocker and accepted the precious bundle from the nurse's hands. "Hey, Princess? You're awake now, aren't you? And very, very hungry." He set the edge of the nipple against the side of the baby's mouth and when she quickly turned and grasped it, he felt as if he'd done something marvelous. "I think she likes when I feed her."

"It would appear so." The nurse's smile said she was half teasing, but Tanner didn't care. To have this beautiful newborn depending on him meant something. No matter what happened, he intended to make sure Princess's life worked out all right.

"And we've got good news," the nurse continued as she restocked diapers and blankets on the nearby trays. "Someone from the family has contacted the social worker. I don't know what that means, but at least this baby isn't completely on her own anymore."

"Family?" Tanner had to push down a note of dread, because Gracie Jayne's existence didn't lend itself to being family friendly. "Her mother's family or her father's family?"

The nurse shook her head. "I'm not sure, the social worker just left a message that we might have visitors on Monday and she'd get back to me with more details. She knows we can't let anyone in here without prior approval of parents or staff, so we'll know more after the weekend."

He started to ask if Julia was aware of this news, but then the nurse added, "And it seems they found a letter in the mother's belongings that stated she wanted Julia Harrison to take charge of her child if Julia was willing."

"Gracie Jayne left a letter?" That was news to Tanner. She'd come across that parking lot with nothing but a thin, worn shoulder bag and the hospital had required him to witness the contents of that bag, then sign his name. There was no letter in the bag. "Where did they find this letter?"

"Some place in the hills. Luke and Seth Campbell came by to see Julia earlier. Of course I don't know any more than that, but with family coming in on Monday, this could get interesting."

"It already has." Tanner stared down at the baby, born bereft. "Has Julia been over here?"

"Twice. And she asked about you, too."

The nurse's grin said she was reading between the lines, but a curl of foreboding hit Tanner, midsection. What if Gracie Jayne's family wanted the baby? What if they weren't the kind of people who should have this child? And what of Gracie Jayne's wishes, that the one person who showed her kindness should have her daughter?

He was jumping to conclusions, but he'd heard the backstory about the Montgomery family. Gracie Jayne hadn't lived up to their expectations and they'd banished her. So what chance would this child have, growing up in similar surroundings? And was a letter worth anything in court? Did Julia want custody of this child, or was the entire scenario a bad scene from a low-rated movie?

The baby squirmed. He stood up and walked her around the small area, patting her back to encourage a burp, and when she offered him a lusty one, he held her out to congratulate her. "Well done! That was a lumberjack-style belch for sure, little girl!"

He didn't know what he expected, but the baby's eyes grew wide. Two tiny eyebrows shot up. And then she seemed to see him, or at least his eyes, and her mouth relaxed into a wide-open smile. Fleeting, yes, but he saw it, and his heart expanded to record proportions. "She smiled at me. Just now." He waved the nurse over. "I was talking to her and I congratulated her on such a good burp and she looked right up at me and smiled!"

"I expect she knows a good thing when she sees it."

Julia's amused voice made him turn. "Is this normal? Do babies smile at people this early?"

"Only the handsome ones," Julia joked. She reached for the baby, took her into her arms and kissed her soft cheek. "You smell so good, sweetie." She looked up at Tanner. "No note?"

"If I get to see you in person, there's no need for a note," he explained. He met her smile with one of his own and reached out to brush loose tendrils of hair back, away from her face, but then his hand lingered there of its own accord. "Did I hear correctly that Gracie Jayne left a letter asking you to take care of the princess?"

She sighed, snuggled the baby and nodded. "But someone from the Montgomery side of the family is coming in on Monday, and I'm going to spend the next forty-eight hours praying for God's will on this whole situation. I always wanted another baby or two," Julia confessed. "I love big families, I love having kids around, so I never understood Vic's reluctance to do things with the boys. What man doesn't want sons to play with? Have a catch with or take to a monster truck show?"

He'd wanted all that and more, and his heart broke when it was denied him, so he was pretty sure Vic was a first-class jerk. Now he wanted Vic's loss to be his gain. A woman like Julia deserved to be loved, honored and cherished all the days of her life, a task he'd like to undertake. "Sacrificial love."

She nodded, emphatic. "Yes. For me it came naturally, but then I realized that a lot of people just don't see it that way."

"They're morons."

She didn't disagree. "But I also know what it's like to long for peace of mind, and what if this person's joy rests on this baby?" She slanted her eyes down to the bundle in her arms. "Maybe loving this child will be their amends to Gracie Jayne? Do I then push a court case on someone because Gracie Jayne was grateful for the little bit of help I offered? Or do I take this as a sign from God that this child is supposed to be mine? Because going to court, fighting others, demanding my rights, well…" She shook her head, her face bemused. "That's just not me."

Her reply was succinct, and she'd most likely hate him more when she found out he was the plaintiff in her associate's suit. Which meant he better go call that lawyer and see about getting his action dropped. "Are you free tonight?"

"No, Sue's got the stomach bug that's going around, so I'm staying right here. I'll catch some sleep before church so I'm in good form for monster trucks."

He hesitated, torn, wanting to spill it all now, get it out in the open, but a glance at the clock said he should be calling his attorney in the next five minutes. "I'll pick you up at one-thirty tomorrow, okay?"

"Bring coffee." She peeked up at him and smiled, and the sight of her, a little mussed after a morning of work, holding the now-sleeping baby, ignited sweet feelings within him. "Cream, sugar—"

"And a shot of caramel."

She laughed softly. "I wouldn't say no."

He leaned down and kissed her forehead, then the baby's cheek, wishing he'd come clean weeks ago. He trudged out of the NICU, went to his car and hit the attorney's number, and when Darren answered, Tanner got right to the point. "I need to withdraw my suit against Southern Erie Women's Medical."

"You what?"

"I need to have the suit dismissed. Withdrawn. Whatever it is you guys do. I don't want to settle, and I don't want to go to court. I just want it over."

The lawyer argued the costs and the time involved, but in the end, he agreed to withdraw the suit against Ashley's doctors and her midwife. "This makes no sense," he told Tanner gruffly, when he finally listened to Tanner's argument and agreed. "To be this close to settlement and pull out. It's a costly mistake, Tanner, and I really think you should take a few days to think about it."

Tanner didn't need any more days. He was done looking back and from now on, the only way he wanted to go was forward. And hopefully...

It would be with Julia and her boys.

"The mistake was in trying to blame someone for what happened," he replied. "Once I made this decision, I slept all night for the first time in three years. And I tell you, it felt good."

"I'll draw up the papers and notify the court on Monday."

"Thank you. And they'll notify the practitioners right away, won't they?"

"I'll send their counsel the letter of withdrawal, as well. The defendants will be informed at that time."

"Good." He'd already caused those people

enough worry. It was time to put things right in all aspects of his life. "Thank you."

"You're welcome. And you know, Tanner," the lawyer hesitated, then said, "I respect what you're doing. I know they were going to settle with us, and I know that most people wouldn't be able to shrug off the lure of that kind of money. I won't deny that I'm feeling the sting myself right now, but I have to say you're one of the few people around who put character ahead of greed."

"It's the right thing to do."

"I'll take care of it."

Tanner hung up the phone, sat back in the driver's seat and stared at the hospital in front of him. He'd made a bold step forward.

Would it bring him a chance to make a life with Julia?

He didn't know.

But from now on, he'd be able to wake up and look at himself in the mirror and not dislike the man he'd become. For that alone, his decision was worth it.

Watching Tanner leave the NICU, a host of options rose before Julia. His open affection for this baby showed what a man was capable of if he loved children. Seeing him hold the newborn, talk to her, rejoice in her, was a refreshing change. She stopped in a small alcove once the baby was asleep. She hadn't heard from the boys, and she'd promised they could call her, so not hearing from them was good, right?

But motherly concern pushed her to dial Vic's number, and when he answered, she didn't waste time exchanging words with him. "Vic, can I speak with Martin, please?"

His drawn-out sigh made her wait long seconds. "Must you? I'm just getting them accustomed to how things work around here. If they talk to you, it's going to mess everything up."

"How can talking to their mother mess up anything? You're being ridiculous. Put Martin on the phone."

"And you're being your typical overprotective self, which is why they have problems in the first place."

Problems?

Concern and worry flashed through her. Martin and Connor didn't have problems. They were normal boys who loved to talk about gross things and climb higher than they should, but that's what boys did. When they weren't pounding on each other. "Put him on, Vic."

"Mommy?" The tremulous note in Martin's

voice made her knees go weak. "Can you come get us?"

She wanted to race three hours across up-state New York and rescue her babies. But she took a deep breath, calming her nerves before trusting herself to speak. "What's going on, honey?"

"I don't think Daddy likes little boys around. Connor's scared."

"Are you scared, honey?"

Martin's intake of breath said he was fighting tears. "I'm trying not to be. There's nothing to do here and our dad says we can't watch TV because it's stupid and it's too wet and cold to play outside, and there are no toys here. I just wanna come home, Mom."

Julia's heart broke into a million pieces. She gripped the phone, fought tears and wondered if judges had any clue what children went through when parents couldn't be trusted. "Put your dad back on, please. And, honey, I love you. I'll pick you guys up tomorrow, and then we'll go to the monster truck show, okay?"

Martin's silence said he couldn't trust himself to speak, and that stirred Julia's protective instincts further. "Wait, before I talk to your father again, let me talk to Connor, okay?"

"'Kay." The muffled voice said he was losing the battle to fight tears, and with Martin, tears had been a common occurrence when he was smaller. He'd gotten tougher this past year, but would forcing him to make these visits reverse his progress?

"Mommy." Connor's pragmatic little voice came on the line and stirred her emotions further. "I miss you. I keep trying not to cry, but then I kind of have to cry because I just want to be with you like all the time," he confessed in a voice that sounded strong and plaintive at the same time. "And I tried to tell my dad that I wanted to call you and he said no, we shouldn't bother you, that you were too busy working and we'd see you tomorrow. So I'm really, really glad you called us because I just wanted to talk to my mom."

Regret pierced Julia.

Was she wrong for moving the boys to Kirkwood? Had she made the decision out of anger or concern? Had her choices put her beloved boys in this awful situation?

"You can talk to me anytime, Connor. Put your father on the phone and I'll make sure he understands that."

"'Kay! Bye, Mom. I love you so much."

"I love you, too, darling. I'll see you tomorrow." She said the words because she had to, when what she wanted was a visual reassurance that the boys were all right. When Vic got back on the phone, she had to count to ten to keep her voice somewhat controlled. "You told them they couldn't call me?"

"I'm preventing them from using you as an excuse to ignore me," he retorted. "We've already had over two years of that."

"Your choice, Vic. Not mine. And furthermore—" She paused as Tanner's words from the night before came back to her. His confession of how he hated the endless war between his parents, the constant drama. But how could she stop this when her emotions were on overload?

You can't. God can. He is the Alpha and the Omega. The one true God. Remember those sweet words you know so well? Come unto me, all who are burdened and weary, and I will give you rest.

She breathed deep as realization swept her. She needed to calm down and prevent their anger from becoming the norm. She thought hard, then noted, "The weather's crummy for doing outside things."

A moment of silence reigned, then Vic replied, "I thought we'd spend time today in the park, but we can't because it's cold and wet. And I have work to do on weekends, it's not like I have all the free time in the world."

She ignored his self-pity speech purposely.

"Do they still have the dinosaur exhibit at the museum?"

He hesitated, then said, "They might. I haven't looked."

"That's always a good rainy day thing. Or one of those indoor play arenas, but they're crammed with kids on a Saturday."

"An indoor playground?" Again a moment of silence stretched long. "They have those?"

"There's an Ithaca family fun website, Vic. I used it on my days off when I lived there. It will tell you where and when things are going on. You can find things to fill this afternoon and evening just by checking it out. Kids never do well with lots of time on their hands."

"You've got that right." He paused again, then breathed deep. "I'll try that when my work's done. See you tomorrow."

No thank you, no gratitude, but at least he said he'd try, and that was a big step forward for Vic because her suggestions had fallen on deaf ears long before their marriage crumbled.

Her pager went off. She moved toward the labor area with mixed emotions. If Vic followed through on his promise, he might be able to salvage the rest of the day. If not, the boys would be miserable and cantankerous.

But they weren't hurt, they weren't in danger and she needed to focus on the positives.

She didn't dare think of Martin fighting tears or Connor's false bravado because right here and now, she needed to focus on the young mother laboring down the hall…

But she'd be lying if she pretended that was an easy thing to do.

Chapter Thirteen

Tanner handed Julia a steaming hot caramel macchiato and jerked his head toward his SUV promptly at one thirty the next afternoon. "Road trip. You and me and these." He held up the four tickets to the truck show and grinned. "I brought earplugs, too. Because I'm that kind of nice."

She laughed, accepted the coffee and climbed into the passenger seat quickly. "I can't wait to see the boys. These have been the two longest days of my life."

"And yet you delivered a baby—"

"Two," she told him. "And then Dr. Matthews took over."

"How did you keep your mind on your work?" He used the curved farm driveway to come back onto the road and turned to face her at the intersection just east of McKinney Farm. "It had to be tough."

"Same as you or anyone, I guess." She sipped her coffee and shrugged. "When I'm with a patient, everything else goes on hold. I tuck my personal life into a little room and shut the door because when I'm delivering a baby, I've got two lives in my hands. I can't afford not to be at the top of my game."

He'd had to do the same thing in his job, but he knew there were times his attention was diverted in the jumble of emotions after losing his family. That's why he'd changed locations, because everything around Erie was a reminder of what he lost. "You go into 'the zone.'"

"Yes. But right now my heart is racing and I can't wait to see my sons. When I talked with them yesterday, I wanted to cry and hit someone at the same time."

"Did you?"

She shook her head and laid her hand on his arm, and the touch of her fingers felt good and right. "No, and that's because of you."

He frowned. "Me?"

"Yup. I remembered what you said about your parents, and I stuffed a virtual sock in my mouth and tried to stow my personal baggage away and handle the situation the way a reasonable person would do it."

He angled a smile of respect her way as he approached the Interstate. "Did it work?"

"It helped." She sipped more of the coffee. "I don't know if he took my advice, but it felt like I was in control of my end of the situation. And that was huge."

"Learning not to fight…" He mulled her situation as the car accelerated. "I think that's a lesson I could use, too."

She poked him. "You're one of the calmest people I know. Quiet. Deep. Maybe too deep sometimes."

He'd tiptoed around her initially because the combination of her occupation and his anger jumbled things.

Now he had his head on straight. And tomorrow her associate should find out that his litigation had been dropped. He opened his mouth to talk with her about it, but her phone rang. She answered quickly, and the smile on her face said it had to be one of the boys. "I'm on my way, too! Tanner and I will meet you guys in an hour." She put them on speakerphone and both boys' voices came through loud and clear.

"Can we get T-shirts? Because I think monster truck T-shirts are cool, Mom!"

"Can I touch the Extreme Dominator?"

"Will we be late?"

"Does Mr. Tanner love big trucks a lot?"

The last question was typical Connor and made Tanner laugh as he answered. "I do, Connor. I've been waiting to go to one of these shows for years, so you guys have given me the best excuse ever. Are we ready to r-r-rumble?" He roared the last word and the shrieks of delighted laughter said his efforts pleased the boys.

"I'm ready!" Martin sounded happy and relieved.

"Me, too!" Connor said.

"I need to focus to drive." Vic's terse voice said he didn't find the conversation all that amusing. "See you in an hour." *Click.*

He hung up before Julia could respond, and she stared at the phone before tucking it away. "That's Vic."

"I heard." Tanner reached over and grasped her hand lightly but kept his eyes on the road. "Wanting to drive safely isn't a bad thing. But that rude voice?" He shrugged it off. "I think he's jealous."

"Jealous? That's silly. We're talking about a man who cheated on me several times. He couldn't care less about what I do."

"You're wrong, and I'll tell you why," Tanner explained. "He's the kind of guy who likes control, so he was okay when *he* was in charge of the situation, making the choices. You changed all that. I expect that's a downright uncomfortable position for him to be in. The boys are happy with you, and you've moved on with your life. That makes controlling guys like him really uncomfortable."

"Does it make me stupid?" The note in her voice said he shouldn't take this question lightly. "To have fallen for a guy who ended up like this? Shouldn't I have seen the signs?"

Tanner shook his head because in his line of work, power-hungry guys were often the toughest to read. "Guys like Vic are good at spinning things, including themselves, any way they want to appear. But they're never satisfied, and no matter what others do, they'll never fill the void inside a guy like that."

"That's how it was." Julia made a face, then shrugged. "And while a part of me would prefer that he stay away and not annoy us, I know the impact of being abandoned by your father can't be good for kids."

"God made kids resilient for a reason," Tanner told her. "And speaking of which, the little princess looked great this morning."

"I stopped by, too, right after church. She seems alert and sweet and absolutely beautiful."

"My thoughts exactly. So what happens tomorrow if Gracie Jayne's family wants her? Have you figured any of this out? Do you want to consult a lawyer?"

"I don't know." She pressed her hands together as she considered the question. "Right now I'm trying to deal mentally with what the boys are going through. Is it foolish to consider throwing a baby into the mix? An unexpected newborn that drops into our laps if Social Services and the courts agree? And the fact that they very well might agree has me examining this from every angle. Would it be in the baby's best interests? And would it shortchange the boys?"

Tanner scoffed at that. "A new baby enriches the family, doesn't it?"

"It should," she agreed. "But generally you have nine months to wrap your head around it. To suddenly have a baby appear on the scene on top of their father's reappearance might mess them up."

"Or teach them to be open to change. And that realization might be the best gift of all."

"You've fallen in love with this baby."

He glanced sideways, saw her arched brow and shrugged the shoulder closest to her. "Guilty."

She sighed. "Me, too. And that's a problem because my plate's already pretty full."

"What about if it was *our* plate, Julia?"

Silence answered him. He glanced sideways again, and the look on her face said she wasn't sure she'd heard correctly. "What if you and I were to make this our family project? You. Me. The boys. The baby. I can't imagine anything that would make me happier than taking that responsibility on with you."

"Are you—?" She gulped, and he nodded.

"Asking you to marry me? Yes. And if you need time, I understand because I know this is quick, but I knew the first night I laid eyes on you, that God put you in my path."

"You weren't exactly God-centered and you were supergrumpy. I'm not sure that first meeting should be a deciding factor."

He laughed because she was 100 percent correct. "I was stubborn and stupid. I've improved. We've got time, Julia, but I wanted you to know what I'm thinking. I'd like a second chance with someone, and I'd like that to be you."

His words stirred her heart, but there was a lot she didn't know about Tanner Reddington. And she couldn't afford a mistake, couldn't risk the boys' well-being, couldn't—

"I was married before."

His quiet voice held her attention.

"We were pregnant with our first child when Ashley went into a sudden cardiac arrest."

Julia's fingers clenched. Her breathing tightened.

Sympathy for Tanner enveloped her because he'd walked a heartbreaking bend in the road no one had seen coming.

"We lost her that day. They delivered the baby by C-section, a tiny little boy named Solomon." The catch in his voice said he still had trouble talking about his loss. "I had him with me for about twelve hours before he joined his mother. And then they were gone. Both gone. In the space of a day I'd lost everything I loved. Everything I cared about. My dreams and my hopes of being a normal family that loved each other just..." He clenched his jaw slightly. "Went away."

Tears filled her eyes. She'd never lost a patient like this, but others had, and the heartbreak of the double loss could shatter souls. "Tanner, I'm so sorry."

He nodded, his chin firm, his gaze forward. "I came to Kirkwood to forget because I couldn't live in a town with all the reminders, but now?" He tipped a glance her way and the surety of his expression sent her heart racing once more. "I want to move ahead. Start over. And in the years since I lost my family, nothing has gotten through to me until that night I met and rescued you. There's a reason for that, Julia, but if you don't feel the same way—"

"I do feel the same."

His jaw relaxed into a quick smile. "Yeah?"

"Yes. Because I think you're right, I don't think our meeting was accidental. I think God's timing has a hand in all of this, and I'd like to talk about this more." She reached over and grasped his right hand as their exit ramp loomed closer. "A lot more, actually. Later. Deal?"

He nodded, winked and steered the car onto the Alfred/Almond exit. "Deal."

He pulled into the parking lot of the convenience store a moment later. Vic's sleek coupe was parked in the shade of the lone tree, engine running. He climbed out of the driver's side, and the boys followed, half falling in their eagerness to see her.

"Mom, you're here!"

"Mom! I missed you so much, like even more than when I leave my bear at Grandpa's!"

"That much?" She buried her face into their combined hugs, then pulled back, laughing. "You look wonderful, boys. Did you have a good weekend?"

Their faces froze. Neither one made eye contact with their father. Connor looked at Martin.

Martin returned the look, then scuffed the toe of his shoe into the gravel with so much force, the rubber toe guard on his sneaker tore. "We tried to," Connor finally answered. Worry creased his little brow. "We rented a movie last night that was really good and I wasn't even hardly scared of the wolves. Mostly."

"Well, good, because it's just a movie and there are no wolves around here. But they sure do make things seem real in the movies, don't they?"

"Yes." Connor nodded hard.

"Very real." The worry in Martin's voice said he could have done with a little less realism.

"Say goodbye to your father, boys, and hop in the backseat. We've got just enough time to get to the truck show."

"Bye."

"Yeah, bye."

Julia stared hard at them, and then they trudged back toward Vic and looked up. "Thank you for having us over." Connor half whispered the words and there was really nothing thankful about his tone or his posture, but he did what he needed to do without a hissy fit, so that was good.

"Thanks, Dad. Sorry I messed up your game station thing."

"I'll get a new one."

Martin nodded, chastised. He walked back to Tanner's SUV and climbed in beside Connor and shut the door.

Julia turned back to Vic to make introductions. "Vic, this is my friend Tanner. Tanner, this is the boys' father, Vic."

"Trooper Tanner." Vic didn't put out his hand, but then, neither did Tanner. "I heard about you." The way he said the words made it sound like he wasn't all that impressed.

But his gaze went sharp when Tanner slung an arm around Julia's shoulders and pulled her closer. "Same here. Thanks for getting the boys back on time. *We* appreciate it."

Tanner started to turn, but Julia hung back. "We need to set things up for spring break."

Vic's expression changed. He raised his hands, palms out. "I'll text you."

Julia nodded. "All right." Relief softened the boys' features when she climbed into the front seat of Tanner's car, and when they'd pulled away from the parking lot, all four of them breathed easier.

Vic didn't wave, and didn't offer a second goodbye. He simply turned, climbed into his car and headed east on the nearby Interstate.

A part of Julia wanted to find out more about their weekend, but her rational side won the mental battle. They talked about trucks, noise, crushers and dominator-style tires and by the time they got the boys' home after the two-hour show, details about the weekend didn't much matter. Had she gotten to have that nice, long talk with Tanner?

No, because two boys and bedtime prevailed, but there was plenty of time for that later. Right now it felt good to have the boys back home with her. They'd made a big step forward, she knew that.

But it had drained her mentally and plain old normal sounded real good.

Tanner answered the lawyer's phone call on Monday morning. "We're all set, papers have been filed, the defendants' attorney has been apprised and the lawsuit is being withdrawn."

Tanner had been waiting for this notification. Now that it came he wasn't sure how he felt. He hoped and prayed he'd done the right thing. He'd been angry at the doctors and midwife for so long, he wasn't sure how to handle this new reality. Did having the lawsuit dismissed mean he'd minimized Ashley's and Solomon's existence?

No.

And yet it felt that way, as if he'd let them down again.

He glanced at his watch, decided he'd forgo lunch later to stop by the hospital and visit Gracie Jayne's baby. No matter what happened, she shouldn't go a day without someone stopping in and holding her. Loving her. Some folks would think he was nuts. They'd say a brand-new baby couldn't discern who was holding her, cuddling her, feeding her, but Tanner didn't care what others thought. It made him feel good to provide that time to a struggling newborn, and that wasn't something he took lightly.

"Did you hear the news?" Miranda Matthews stopped into Julia's office midmorning. "Your buddy has dropped his lawsuit against me."

"My who has done what?" Julia stared up at Miranda, perplexed. "I have no idea what you're talking about, Miranda."

"Your new guy, Tanner Reddington?"

"My friend Tanner," Julia corrected her, but from the rise of heat in her cheeks, she was pretty sure Miranda wasn't fooled a minute.

"Okay." Miranda put her hands up and made air quotes with her fingers. "Your *friend* Tanner has dropped the lawsuit he filed against my old practice. I just got a call from our attorney."

Julia's heart tripped and fell. She tried to

wrap her head around Miranda's statement, but it wasn't computing. "Tanner was suing you?"

"Yes." Miranda sank down into the chair opposite Julia, chagrined. "You didn't know?"

Julia shook her head. "How would I? You've never mentioned a name—"

"Privacy rules. I never met him, but I recognized the name when someone said he was helping at the clinic. His wife was attended by our midwife—"

Julia's heart shrank. Tanner had lost his wife and son, a fact she'd just learned…

Then sued the midwife taking care of her. "What were the grounds of the lawsuit?"

"Gross negligence and failure to act."

Her heart raced. This was the scenario every OB doctor and midwife hated. In obstetrics, there was no second place trophy. You either won the race and delivered a child or you suffered dire consequences. There was no in-between, and she'd listened to the ache in Tanner's voice yesterday, knowing how he must have felt, but unaware he was suing Miranda's former team for malpractice.

"Anyway, the suit's been dropped. The insurance company was going to settle this week, before the court date." She stood. "Now we don't have to. I don't want to bring up such a sore topic with the guy, and I had no idea he lived here in Kirkwood when I relocated here, but I'm grateful for what he's done. The whole thing was heartbreaking, but totally unpredictable. It couldn't have been an easy decision for him to make because the insurance company was prepared to make a six-figure settlement. Tanner Reddington answered a lot of prayers today by making this go away."

"I'm sure he did." Julia uttered the simple words, but the pressure inside her chest mushroomed. No wonder he'd acted weird around her when they first met. And his reaction to the pregnancy clinic?

Understandable in hindsight.

But to keep this from her said he either didn't trust her, didn't trust midwives or didn't trust anyone, and how could she lose her heart to another man who kept secrets? Love was nothing without trust, so this precious emotion she'd been nurturing for Tanner was obviously not returned the same way.

She'd trusted him.

He'd hidden his deepest feelings away.

Her private line buzzed, the hospital calling. "Julia Harrison, how can I help you?"

"Julia, it's Wanda. I wanted to tell you that Gracie Jayne Montgomery's mother intends to put in a formal request for custody of her granddaughter."

She'd expected this. Assumed it was coming, because how could anyone who might have ever loved Gracie Jayne turn their back on her innocent child? But if this was the best thing for the baby, wouldn't Gracie Jayne have indicated that? If she trusted her family even the littlest bit, wouldn't she have turned to them at some point? And why get Julia involved at all, other than as a medical practitioner, if the baby was going to be awarded to the very people who banished Gracie Jayne from the family?

"...as we forgive those who trespass against us..."

She recited the familiar passage from the Lord's Prayer often, but right now the meaning tread harshly on her soul. She'd forgiven often in her life, the warmth of charity calmed her soul, but to learn of Tanner's duplicity and then receive Wanda's phone call?

She wanted to curl up someplace and cry, except she couldn't. What had she told Tanner yesterday? That when everything went bad, she had to put it into a locked mental compartment and throw away the key because she had a job to do, a job of bringing life into the world.

And that's exactly what she did. Tanner's lies went on one side, Gracie Jayne's antagonistic family went on the other and she locked away the emotions both stirred. It was Holy Week, a week of commemorating Christ's triumphant ride into Jerusalem and then his trial and death. A week rife with emotion for believers.

Right now this week was proving to be rife with emotion for multiple reasons.

Chapter Fourteen

Tanner called Julia midafternoon. The call went to voice mail, not unusual for her busy workdays. "Julia, can I come by tonight once the boys are in bed and have that talk we mentioned yesterday? Let me know if that works for you. Oh, and I just stopped to see the baby. I met her grandmother." He tried to hold back the sigh, but couldn't quite do it. "We need to talk about that, too."

She didn't return his call. She didn't text him. And when he finished his shift and double-checked to make sure his phone was on, it was. And still no word from Julia.

He texted her then because maybe the voice mail function wasn't working properly. "Can we talk tonight? I can bring pizza."

No reply.

He climbed into his car and pulled into

Marty Harrison's driveway fifteen minutes later. The door burst open and Connor raced down the steps to greet him, wearing his new The Extreme Dominator Rules!!! T-shirt from the monster truck show. "Mr. Tanner, everyone thought my shirt was the coolest one in school today and my teacher said my show-and-tell was really exciting to hear!"

Tanner laughed and scooped him up. "I expect it was, but it's a little chilly to be running outside without a sweatshirt, isn't it?"

"Not if it's just for like a minute," Connor explained and the earnest tone of voice made Tanner smile. "For just a minute it's okay, Mom says."

"Well, Mom's pretty smart," Tanner admitted, and when he looked up, Julia was framed in the door, watching them. Sadness blanched her features when their eyes met, but when Connor turned and jumped out of Tanner's arms, all traces of angst vanished and she greeted the boy with a big, broad smile.

Connor dashed off, the overgrown pup barked halfheartedly at Tanner, then trotted after the boy to the lower family room level, leaving Tanner and Julia alone. He stepped in, even though he wasn't asked, and when he did, she took a firm step back, arms folded tight around her middle.

Uh-oh. "I called you earlier."

She nodded, but said nothing and another warning bell sounded. "And then I texted you."

"You did."

He studied her for a few seconds, then frowned, confused. "I was hoping we could sit down and have that talk we put off yesterday once the boys are in bed tonight, but I'm sensing I'm in trouble and I'm not sure what I've done. Care to enlighten me?"

"You were suing Miranda."

She'd heard about the lawsuit, and the fact that she hadn't heard it from him made it bad. "Yes."

"Actually, let me get this right," she went on. "You were suing her and her whole practice including the midwife your wife had picked as her primary."

His fingers tightened. His knuckles ached. "I was. And now I'm not. It's pretty simple, really. I wanted to blame someone for what happened. God and Ashley's obstetrical practice got the brunt of my anger. I know that doesn't make it right, but you're a medical professional, Julia. I expect you've seen the different ways people handle grief before, haven't you?"

"I don't do secrets, Tanner."

"I should have told you sooner."

"But you didn't, and I made a pledge when I moved here that I would never allow myself to be put in a compromising position. The lack of trust and respect—" She winced as if pained. "I won't ever let that be part of my life again."

"It's not like that, Julia." He took a step forward and she took two steps back, then pointed at the door.

"Love without trust is not a mistake I intend to repeat. It's not the fact that you were suing their practice," she continued, her gaze hard. "That's your legal right. It's the fact that you hid it from me for weeks and I had to hear it from a colleague, a colleague who wants you to know she's grateful for the reprieve."

So the doctor appreciated his change of heart, but Julia, the woman who'd managed to lay claim to that same heart, had lost faith in him.

"Mr. Tanner! Mr. Tanner, can you stay and play with us? Mom's making supper and we could do smash-up-derby car crashes on the floor. Grandpa's floor makes the cars go super fast!"

He turned and the sweet, earnest look from Julia's youngest son made him long to stay, but the blank expression on Julia's face said he'd lost that right. "Wish I could, bud. I've got stuff to do tonight."

"Maybe another time?" Connor moved forward quickly and grasped Tanner's hand, and with that touch, grabbed his heart, as well. "I'll keep everything all picked up so you can come play with us, okay?"

His throat went tight. His face ached with false cheer. His chest felt hard and stiff, as if the weight of a thousand anvils sat firm against his breastbone. "You do that. See you later, okay?" He crouched down and Connor threw himself into Tanner's arms.

"I'll be super good. Martin, too. That way we can do cool stuff together soon, okay?"

"Okay."

He turned to go, wishing she'd reconsider. Ask him to stay. Understand that he hadn't meant to hurt people, he'd just…

Just what? Wanted to share the pain? Spread the agony out? Make everyone suffer?

He shook off the thoughts as he pushed through the door.

He pulled onto the road, heart heavy. Julia's face had been so untrusting and sad. So sad. Connor had been so excited, then disappointed. Even the big pup had looked confused when he left, as if hoping to have a little time together, then thwarted by emotions he didn't understand.

He longed to talk to somebody. Someone

who wouldn't think he was a terrible jerk and a no-good, very bad person for hating his life when Ashley and little Sol died.

Marty's truck was parked down the road outside the McKinney Farm barn. He hesitated, then pulled into the farm drive and parked next to Marty's rugged pickup. Julia's father might hate him for letting this happen, but on the other hand, no one in Kirkwood would understand his change of heart better than Marty. He strode into the barn as Marty and Piper's uncle finished wiping down a newborn calf with straw ticks.

"You're in some deep trouble, son." Marty straightened, rolled his shoulders and continued ministrations to the new little bull. "I do believe I warned you not to break her heart."

"You did, sir. And yet I managed to mess up anyway."

"Hmm." Marty scowled, then stroked a gentle hand along the calf's spine. "He seems sound, Berto. And nice conformation. He'll do well at market." He turned back to Tanner, jerked his head for Tanner to follow him and walked across the barn to the scrub sink alongside the milking parlor. He turned the water on, let it get hot, then started scrubbing up. "So you messed up your timing royally. Now what?"

Tanner wasn't quite sure. "Grovel?"

"A good start." An almost smile softened Marty's jaw. "I see heartbreak waiting to happen all around Julia these days. That baby waiting on a home in Clearwater, the boys being pushed into a situation we can't change and one that they hate, the contractor is messing up the time frame on fixing her house and now she gets to toss heartbreak over you onto the already smoking fire."

"She deserves to be happy."

Marty scoffed, wiped his hands and cuffed Tanner's arm. "It's not about what we deserve, it's about God wanting us happy. Tanner, if you just step back and look at this situation right now, all of it, what will it take to make Julia happy?"

He frowned. "Me?"

"Got it in one!" Marty wiped his arms and hands with a clean towel, then tossed it into the soiled towel bin next to the sink. "Woo her. Court her. Make her smile the way a woman likes to smile, then you marry her and make her happy. And if you don't, I'll be the first in line to mop the floor with you, okay?"

"You think she'll forgive me?"

Marty rolled his eyes. "Julia's been happier the last few weeks than I've seen her in years, so yes, she'll forgive you. After you grovel, of course. I'd start with flowers, if it was me, but then I'm probably out of touch with what women like."

His phone rang just then, and Tanner had no trouble telling it was Laura on the other end. Marty winked and said, "So you liked the flowers all right?" Tanner had to smile.

He waved goodbye, and when Marty laughed at something Laura said, Tanner recognized the emotion. It was the sound of love through laughter, an emotion he was determined to bring back to Julia, no matter what it took.

She'd faked being happy last night because the boys were there. And she'd put on a smiling face this morning for the same reason. But as Julia slipped into the NICU midday, she didn't want to smile. She wanted to cry because her life had turned upside down in a few short weeks. She picked up the baby, then settled into the rocking chair next to her crib. The infant's scent filled her. The soft breathing, the steady heartbeat, the occasional tweaks and jerks of a small but healthy newborn, all spoke to her.

This baby was a blessing, regardless of how she'd come into the world. She was a gift from God, a tiny human in need of tender, loving care.

She leaned back, rocking the baby, praying, wondering what exactly Gracie Jayne had wanted for this child, because more than anything else, shouldn't a mother's wishes take precedence? She must have dozed off because the next thing she heard was the soft voice of the nurse calling her name. "Julia? Are you asleep?"

She had been, but she pretended she wasn't. She opened her eyes, but it wasn't just Amy, the current nurse standing in front of her. A woman stood next to her, an older woman, well into her sixties by Julia's estimation, and very well dressed. She studied Julia for several seconds, and when Amy brought a second rocker over to the baby's curtained area, the older woman took a seat.

"Julia, this is Eloise Montgomery, Gracie Jayne's mother. Mrs. Montgomery, this is the midwife who helped your daughter."

Julia started to sit more upright, but the baby squeaked a protest, so she leaned back again, unsure what to say. How did one start a conversation about a deceased child, an unexpected grandchild and a family torn by dissension?

"I wanted to meet you." Mrs. Montgomery sat upright in the chair, a position that seemed to fit her pretty hair, polished nails and the stylish long, floral dress. "To thank you. I planned on coming over to your office tomorrow."

Julia waved off the praise. "There are no thanks needed. I was in the right place at the right time and God set your daughter down in front of me. It was perfect timing."

The woman's face said yes and no. "You were in the right place because you're initiating health services to help people in need. You got word out, so women would hear. You're making the women's health clinic happen, and if you hadn't done that, my daughter would have probably died in the hills, and this baby would have succumbed with her. I know this because I went back and checked you out to see what kind of person you are. And what I saw was quite impressive, young lady."

"Well, I—"

Mrs. Montgomery leaned forward, and the mix of emotions said she had a lot on her plate, a situation Julia understood well. "I am to blame for a lot of what happened with Gracie Jayne. I know that now, too late, of course, but I didn't understand back then, that people react to all the wrong things."

"Human nature can be both sensitive and sensitized," Julia agreed.

A frown darkened the older woman's eyes.

Her hands clenched the folds of her dress, causing wrinkles that flowed over her knees like floral ribbons, cascading. "I hated my mother. She was a mean, cruel woman and she left scars that have lasted forever. What kind of mother does that? I wondered. But then I had Gracie Jayne, she was my second child, and she looked just like my mother." Nerves elongated her syllables, and the wrinkles in the gown grew more defined. "I couldn't look at her and not see my mother. And when she started to talk, most mothers would have been thrilled, because she was so smart, so bright! Me?" She shook her head, her attention centered on the newborn in Julia's arms. "All I heard was Alice Henry Wainwright, my mother, and it was as if God played a dirty trick on me, putting my mother right back into my life after I'd finally escaped."

Julia gripped the baby tighter as fear crawled up her spine. What kind of life did Gracie Jayne have with this woman? What kind of mother doesn't cling to their child and recognize their individuality?

"You probably think I'm a horrid person, and I was. I turned my back on my child because I couldn't deal with the past and I made her life miserable." She lifted her eyes to Julia's and sighed. "Emotional trauma is a difficult thing to see in ourselves. I thought I'd done all right, I'd gotten away from my mother and I was married with two kids and financially blessed. I didn't understand that Gracie's resemblance was nothing more than genetics because I couldn't deal with my past. The poor child never stood a chance with me, and that was my fault. Not hers. I didn't start to see things differently until she got into trouble. I came to realize that I was the problem. Not her. By then it was too late to make a difference. I know God has forgiven me, but I can't even begin to forgive myself. And now there's this child." She settled a soft look on the sleeping baby. "A gift from God."

Julia clutched the baby closer. The image of Gracie Jayne came back to her. So much time lost, love wasted. She remembered her heartache over losing her tiny, baby girl. The months of joyful anticipation gone in a second trimester miscarriage. And as much as she loved her boys, the loss of that pregnancy left a gap within her. But was she as guilty as the woman before her, wanting to use this infant to soothe old hurts? Maybe.

Gracie Jayne's mother gazed at the baby and her winsome expression made her look softer. Younger. "I came in here last night, knowing exactly what I needed to do."

"And that was?"

"To make up for what I messed up before." The older woman's face shadowed. "To show this baby the love and devotion that never reached her mother."

Julia assessed the woman before her. She seemed quiet, polite and sincere, and more up-scale than Julia had imagined. She appeared to be emotionally stable now, but was she? How could Julia know?

"I know my daughter left a letter asking you to take this child."

"Yes."

"And I can see by your face that you love her."

Julia didn't pretend otherwise. "It would be hard not to fall in love with a precious baby like this. Orphaned at birth, no name, no family to welcome her into the world. But she has family now," Julia continued. "You're here, and that makes things different, doesn't it?"

"It does." Contemplation smoothed Mrs. Montgomery's features. "May I hold her?"

"Of course." Julia slipped out of the comfortable rocker carefully, then settled the sleeping baby into her grandmother's arms. "Does she look like Gracie Jayne did as a baby?"

Mrs. Montgomery studied the newborn's face, then shook her head. "Not really, but she does look like her uncle Sean. My son, Gracie Jayne's older brother. He's got a very Irish look about him, and I think she does, too."

"Celt, for sure." Julia laid her hand on the baby's shoulder, then straightened. "I need to get back to work because as nice as it would be to rock her all day, I've got half a dozen afternoon appointments that might be irked if I don't get to the office on time." She leaned down and kissed the baby's soft cheek. "You enjoy this time with your granddaughter, Mrs. Montgomery."

"I will." The older woman nodded as she held the infant close, but then she tipped her gaze back up to Julia's. "May we talk more? Soon?"

"Absolutely." Julia started for the exit, but Mrs. Montgomery reached out a hand to Julia's arm, pausing her. When Julia turned back, bright tears pooled in the old woman's eyes, then spilled, slipping silently onto the sleeping child below. "Did she suffer, Ms. Harrison? My Gracie Jayne? Before she died?" Anguish marked her face. Liquid remorse left tracks along her cheeks.

Julia squatted, met her gaze and gripped her hand. "No. Not at all. She was brave right through till the end. Her goal was to give this baby a chance at life, and that's exactly what she did. You'd have been proud of her, Mrs. Montgomery."

Raw emotion shook the woman's shoulders, but she nodded, and when she did, her chin firmed. "I am proud of her. More than she'll ever know. You're young and you've got a lot of life ahead of you, young lady, but whatever you do, whatever comes your way, don't make the mistakes I made. There's always a time to forgive unless we let anger block the way."

Her words brought Julia up short. *Unless we let anger block the way...*

She walked away, considering the truth of those words. She'd let anger and resentment against Vic smolder inside her. She'd put on a face for the boys, but bitterness dug deep within. And she'd been a little bit happy that his weekend with the boys was a bust, but that was her selfishness talking.

Unless we let anger block the way... Forgive us our trespasses as we forgive those who trespass against us...

God's words, Christ's instruction. She was guilty of talking the talk, but she'd failed at walking the walk. Forgiveness. Healing. Faith.

Head down, she headed to her car, went to work and prayed between each patient. She'd played the victim in some ways and rose to the occasion in others, but she had let pride cling to anger, and that wasn't the person she wanted to be. No matter what happened with the baby, she wanted to be the loving, giving person she used to be, inside and out.

A package sat on the front steps when she pulled into the driveway ten minutes before the boys' bus would appear. She walked over, picked it up and the bright, spring floral paper reminded her of the upcoming Easter celebration. With Holy Week upon them, it was a time of contemplation, prayer and sacrifice, remembering what Christ had done for all mankind.

She opened the gift. A small card tumbled into her lap. She picked it up and read the message scrawled on one side.

My sister Neda sent me this book three years ago. I ignored it for way too long, but when I finally pulled it out to read, it helped me heal. I want to share it with you today, Julia.
With love,
Tanner.

She opened the box and a book commemorating Mother Teresa's life of sacrifice sat in folds of paper. The first quote jumped out at her. "Peace begins with a smile."

A tiny truth, yet so poignant. She sank onto

the step and read the thin book of quotes cover to cover, waiting for the boys. When they raced up the drive a few minutes later, she was able to count her blessings. She was healthy, strong, financially secure and her children were amazing. God had been good to her, so good! What human element made her cling to old resentment and hurt feelings?

The sun burst through the thick spring clouds as the boys led the way inside, bathing the first golden daffodils in bright, warm light and brightening her soul the same way.

"Mom, can we come with you to help at the clinic tonight?" Martin put his math homework sheet on the table and looked up. "I can get this done in no time," he bragged, and while she loved his growing self-confidence, a little boy's bedtime and their upcoming clinic opening didn't allow her much leeway that evening. "And then I can help you paint."

"I appreciate the offer, but you're with Grandpa tonight because Sunday night kind of messed up our sleep around here. A couple of nights of normal is in everyone's best interests, kiddo."

"But it was so fun!" Connor grinned at her from the couch and splayed the picture of the Extreme Dominator on his shirt again. "And I have to ask Grandpa to wash this so I can wear it again tomorrow. Or I can just wear it like this," he supposed, looking down at mac-and-cheese stains across the midsection. "No one cares."

"I care." Julia stuck out her hand. Connor peeled off the shirt and she started a quick load of laundry. "Grandpa can throw it into the dryer later. Are you intending to wear it all week?"

"Yes." Connor said. "It's the best shirt ever. And do we have to go to Dad's house next week? It's our week off, and we think we should be able to stay here and play, Mom."

Julia turned from the sink, because the voice was Connor's but the words were pure Martin, and it wasn't the first time he'd duped his younger brother into saying what the older brother thought. As she sliced potatoes into a pan, she replied, "You need to get to know your dad, and he has the right to get to know you. He doesn't have school next week, neither do you, and it's a good opportunity to have time together."

Martin stared down at the math and his pencil didn't move an inch.

Connor stuck out his lower lip, plunked himself into Grandpa's favorite chair and scowled. "I want to stay here. With you. That's my favorite thing!"

It was hers, too, but Mrs. Montgomery's words came rushing back... *Unless we let anger block the way...* "Your dad loves you, and I know your weekend wasn't the best, but it's hard to try new things. For you—" she pointed at Connor "—and you—" she directed her gaze at Martin "—and your father. Give it a chance, boys. Your dad's a good soccer player and he loves fast cars and he's not too far from the Watkins Glen speedway. Maybe he'll take you there."

"To a car race?" Connor slipped off the couch with new purpose. "For real?"

"I love fast cars," Martin admitted, and he looked a little more intrigued. "And now that the sun is coming out sometimes, the cars can start racing again."

"Exactly." She smiled at them. "I'll call your father and suggest it, okay?"

The boys nodded as Marty came in the side door, shucked off his barn coat and sniffed. "I smell nothing."

She laughed and pushed a package of burgers into his hands. "I'm working at the clinic to do that final coat of paint on the waiting room, the potatoes are ready to cook and the sun is shining so burgers on the grill it is." She kissed each boy goodbye as she moved to the door. "I probably won't get back until nine, so I'll see you guys in the morning."

"See ya." Marty gave her a casual wave, but she noticed a gleam in his eye when he smiled her way. "Think you'll be ready for an Easter Monday grand opening?"

The boys would be in Ithaca, tiptoeing into their new relationship with their dad, so yes, she was looking forward to the added workload of that first opening week. "Yes, thanks to all the volunteer efforts. Love you, Dad."

"You, too, kid."

She pulled into the clinic fifteen minutes later, unlocked the door and flicked the light switch to her right. Bright new fixtures lit the freshly finished walls. Flooring had been laid in the back hall and the examining rooms, but the reception area was waiting for them to complete this one last coat of paint before the floor guys continued into the waiting room.

Piper had promised to help apply the yellow paint, but she hadn't arrived yet. Julia placed her jacket and purse behind the receptionist's counter and set to work. She turned when the sound of the front door opening announced Piper's arrival, only it wasn't Piper Harrison standing there, looking at her.

It was Tanner.

Her heart leaped.

He stood there, standing straight and tall, then shrugged off his jacket, set it next to hers and rolled up his sleeves. "You're staring."

"Because you're not supposed to be here. Piper is. She promised."

He proceeded to pull out a second tray for rolling paint. "Do you want to cut in with the brush and I roll? Or vice versa?"

"Tanner, I—"

"Or..." He faced her as if mulling something very important and whispered, "We could just kiss and make up and live happily ever after." He laid one big hand along the curve of her cheek. "Because that would be my first choice."

She started to talk, but he put one finger against her mouth. "First let me apologize. I didn't mean to blindside you. The first night I found you here, I hated the thought of this clinic being right under my nose, day after day. On top of that, it was going to be staffed by a midwife, reminding me of everything I'd lost. But the truth is that this clinic, and meeting you, was the best thing that ever happened to me, Julia. I was so mired down in anger and loss and getting even that I forgot to just be me. And once I started to finally get a clue, I didn't know how to tell you."

"That's when you canceled the lawsuit."

He nodded. "Yes. And I should have done it long ago because it wasn't about the money to me. Not ever. It was about admitting they'd done something wrong, and paying for their mistake. But when I realized they'd settle even if they had done nothing wrong, my conscience kicked in. I knew that wasn't the kind of man I wanted to be, or the kind of man God wanted me to be."

"And now?"

His hand caressed her cheek softly. "I want your forgiveness. I want a second chance. I want to love and be loved. I want to wrestle with those boys and take them to see cool things and wake up each morning next to you. Unless you're on call," he amended with a smile, "and need to leave in the middle of the night. In that case, I'd request that you don't wake us up because tired boys are cranky creatures."

She reached up and laid her fingers over Tanner's. "I like the sound of that, too."

"Really?" He smiled down at her, into her eyes, and then his left hand cradled the other side of her face. "Because I have more convincing arguments ready, if necessary."

That sounded intriguing and downright nice. "Care to show me?"

"Yes," he whispered, and dropped his mouth

to hers. His hands lingered on her cheeks for long moments before he drew her into his arms and deepened the kiss.

Being in Tanner's arms, wrapped in his embrace, was a blessing she thought she'd lost, but no. She'd just mislaid it. "I love the book you sent." She whispered the words against his T-shirt-clad chest when he hauled her in for a long, warm hug. "It's beautiful."

"Neda sent it to me a long time ago and I was so mad I shoved it into a drawer and refused to look at it. Once I took the time to read it, I realized I'd been foolish and I didn't want to be a jerk anymore."

"Grieving doesn't make you a jerk." She met his eyes. "It's part of healing."

"Well, I took it to extremes, but I learned a lot, too, Julia." He smiled down at her. "I'd been surrounded by anger all my life, and I carried that into my grief. No more. I promised God I'd move beyond those old ways. Families need joy and smiles. Discipline, too, but mostly? Joy and smiles."

She'd reached the same conclusion. Coincidence? No. God's perfect timing. She pulled Tanner down for one more kiss, then sighed. "We need to paint."

"We do."

"Time for kisses later."

"One can only hope."

She laughed. Laughing with Tanner seemed like something she could do forever. She eased out of his arms, grabbed the brush and said, "I'll cut in around the corners. You can roll."

"Got it. And we're still on for Easter egg hunt, aren't we? I stopped to see if Reverend Smith needed help, and he said between the McKinneys, Harrisons and the Campbells, it was pretty well covered."

"It will be wonderful." She climbed two steps up the ladder and smiled over her shoulder. "Your first Easter egg hunt."

"With you and the boys." He sent a lazy grin her way as he filled his roller with paint. "This will be the best Easter ever."

It would, she decided. God's plan, his timing, Tanner's love. No matter what else happened in her life, she'd start counting her blessings more because they were sweet and abundant.

Chapter Fifteen

Vic's number flashed as Julia hurried the boys out the door on Saturday morning. She longed to let the call go to voice mail. She answered because it was the right thing to do "Vic, hey. We're on our way to an Easter egg hunt so I only have a minute. Can I call you back midday?"

"Sure, but this will only take a minute."

"Well, then…go for it."

"About the boys next week…"

"Yes?"

"I can't take them the whole week. In fact, I can't take them the weekend, either, I got this new job as principal of the middle school starting in July and I've got to focus my time on that. I'm not sure how to keep the boys happy while I'm working—"

"But you're off next week, aren't you?" she

wondered. "You have the same spring break we do."

"Technically yes, but I'll be expected to know the job when it starts, and I figured I'd spend this week checking out the middle school, the scheduling, the problems. So I'm swamped. Is it a problem for you to keep them?"

A problem? As if. She kept her voice easy. "Of course not. Did you want me to plan on your weekend in April?"

"Let's wait on that. If I'm basically working two jobs, that might not work, either."

She bit her tongue and sent up a tiny prayer that someday, somehow he'd see the amazing blessing of his sons, but at least he wasn't leaving them in suspense about his intentions. "Vic, I really appreciate the heads-up. And you know, you'll have more time this summer, the weather allows you more things to do outside, and the boys share your love for fast cars and racing. Maybe you could start there? Take them for a few days then, and just go outside and have fun with them."

"They like racing?" His voice held a note of hope that she hadn't heard from Vic in a very long time.

"Love it. And with the Glen so close..."

"I'll check my calendar and plan on it. And, Julia? Thanks."

She breathed deeply, because even if they weren't on common ground, at least they'd put the emotional weapons aside. "No problem. Happy Easter, Vic."

"Oh. Yeah. You, too."

She hung up the phone and climbed into the car, then faced the boys behind her. She purposely kept it simple. "Your dad has to work next week, so you can't go there, but he'd like to take you to the racetrack this summer. Sound good?"

Martin looked at Connor. He tried to stifle his grin, but Connor didn't even make an attempt. He fist pumped the air and shrieked, "We get to stay home with Mom!"

Martin's grin spread, but then he looked at Julia. "I think I'd like to go to the racetrack this summer, though. I remember that Dad loves fast cars. Just like me."

"Me, too!" Not to be outdone, Connor let it be known that he was in favor of the racetrack trip. "I love smash-up derbies the best!"

"Well, all right." Julia backed out of the turnaround and aimed for the road. "But right now, let's get to this Easter egg hunt, okay?"

"Drive, Mom! Drive fast!"

"I'm on it, kid." She pulled into the overflow parking lot by the old church hall, and the first person she saw was Tanner. He moved their way, and his smile said she was special. *They* were special. That he cared for her just the way she was.

"I brought this." He handed her a to-go cup from Tina's Corner Café and swept a sweet kiss to her mouth, right there, in front of everyone. "Good morning, beautiful."

Heat tinged her cheeks, but she met his smile with one of her own and touched her hand to his cheek. "Morning. And thank you."

"Julia?"

She turned when she heard the reverend's voice. He moved her way, and by his side was Gracie Jayne's mother, Eloise Montgomery. "Mrs. Montgomery." Julia reached out and grasped the other woman's hand. "Is there something wrong? Is the baby all right?"

"Fine. She's fine, dear." She offered her hand to Tanner, but did Tanner simply take her hand? No. He reached out and gave the older woman a big hug. Her face said the unexpected gesture left her surprised, but pleased and when he released her, she righted her hat and turned toward the reverend. "I came to see Reverend Smith this morning. I never thought to make an appointment, but he was gracious enough to talk to me."

"About?"

Mrs. Montgomery turned her way. "You, actually. I was sitting in the hospital last night, holding that perfectly beautiful baby, and I started thinking. I'm sixty-eight years old, not the age of a typical mother, but certainly the age of a doting grandmother."

Julia's heart started beating faster. Stronger.

"Frankly, I did the math. My heart longs to raise that child, but my head said that eighty-six years old is no time to be sending a child off to college. But I want, no, *need*," she stressed the word and took Julia's hands into her own, "to be part of her life. Julia, I've heard nothing but glowing things about you, from the people in your life, and I hope you're not insulted that I checked."

"When it comes to the welfare of a child? I think checking is the very best thing to do," Julia replied. "Are you saying you will allow me to raise her?"

"She means 'us,' of course," Tanner interjected, and he put an arm around Julia's shoulders as he stressed the pronoun. "Mrs. Montgomery, we'd like you to allow *us* to adopt Gracie Jayne's baby because nothing would make me happier than being married to this woman and raising these kids. And any others God might see fit to send us," he added, smiling.

"Yes." Eloise locked eyes with Julia and took a step forward. "I don't want Gracie Jayne's last wish to be disrupted. It would be wrong to do so. And this way, I can relax and be the baby's grandmother, if that's all right—"

"All right? It would be wonderful!" Julia embraced the older woman, and when she felt Eloise's tears, she hung on tight. "She'll love having a grandma close by, and you've just made a beautiful day even more special, Eloise. I think—" she stepped back and looked into the older woman's eyes "—Gracie Jayne would be proud."

"This baby needs a name." Tanner cut right to the chase and he studied both women.

"Well, I hate my first name, so please take that out of the running," Eloise told them. "I'd always wished people would call me Mary, my middle name, but my mother wouldn't hear of it."

"Mary." Tanner looked down at Julia and she looked right back.

"Mary Jayne," she offered, and he nodded.

"It's perfect."

"It is." She hugged him, hugged him hard, and when he handed her a wad of tissues from

Tina Campbell's purse, she laughed and wiped her face. "Happy tears are the best."

His smile said he didn't disagree. "Can we take the boys to meet her after the egg hunt?"

"The egg hunt! I forgot all about it!" Julia turned and realized the entire congregation had been gathering behind her. "Yes, absolutely, we can take them to meet her. And then…" She lifted her eyes to Tanner's. "We need to make plans."

He grinned. "Quick plans, I hope."

She met his grin with a smile of understanding and love. "Very quick. But first—"

"The Easter egg hunt."

"Yes. Eloise, would you like to stay?"

"I'd love to."

Julia took her arm. They stood together on the side of the old church hall gathering yard and watched as children of all ages went to their designated spots. And when the ringing bell said it was time to hunt, boys and girls scoured the hillside leading to the shaded cemetery, squealing with delight each time they came across a filled plastic egg.

"I'd forgotten how much fun this was," the older woman whispered, her gaze darting back and forth. "I think somewhere along the way, I forgot to have fun at all."

Julia hugged her arm gently. "Then we start today, Eloise."

The boys charged their way, balancing baskets filled with brightly colored eggs. Tanner high-fived them, and Eloise bent low, admiring each and every egg and the sight of them filled Julia with new satisfaction. A family—her family—brought from God's elements, in His time.

Perfect.

Epilogue

"How's she doing?" Julia tiptoed across the living room in late May, a half hour before the boys were due home from school.

"Sleeping. Eating. Smiling." Tanner reached up and tugged Julia down to the recliner. "She's amazing. Beautiful. And she loves me."

"Well, who doesn't?"

He laughed, handed the sleeping baby to Julia and kissed them both. "I need coffee. I dozed off cuddling her so we napped together."

"The best kind of nap," Julia whispered. She settled back in the recliner and snuggled the sleeping newborn against her chest. "Tell me again how blessed we are."

Tanner's smile said he didn't need words. "Your dad and Laura are making supper. And

Eloise is coming over. The boys want to show her the cows."

"She'll love it. Except for the mud and the smell."

Tanner laughed, brought her coffee to the side table and crouched low. "I think we're good for her. And she's good for us. And you, Julia Reddington?"

"Yes?" She smiled as he leaned in to kiss her.

"You've made me the happiest man in the world. Thank you."

"Well, the feeling's mutual, darling, but it is your turn to get up tonight, so don't try and sweet-talk your way out of it."

He laughed, palmed Mary Jayne's little head and kissed her sweet, soft cheek. "It will be my pleasure. Just make the morning coffee extra strong, okay?"

"Deal."

The school bus rumbled to a stop outside. Tanner went to run interference at the door, but if two wonderful, rowdy boys managed to wake their baby sister up?

There were plenty of adults around to take care of her, and that was the blessing of family close by.

Marty came in the side door to make supper, but had to peek in at the baby first. Laura followed him with a big tray of lasagna, and Tanner suspected she'd become Grandma Laura before too long.

And when Eloise came in with a box of Popsicles for the whole crew, Tanner knew he was in for the summer of his life.

And it felt wonderful.

* * * * *

Dear Reader,

Julia's story was inspired about two years ago when I wandered onto Angela Ruth Strong's blog and saw her tackle the problems of the rejected spouse. Her words made me look at the what-ifs of the situation. How do children handle the breakup? How do family members deal with the philandering and estranged spouse? How does a woman repair the damage to a fragile ego when the person she loves most strays into another woman's arms?

I brought all of this into Julia's story, a story of today's young mother, a professional woman, skilled, beloved and respected…and how she puts the pieces back together over time.

But then, who to pair her with? That had to be Tanner, a man who lost it all in one short day. No one expects to lose a wife to pregnancy complications these days, but when the unthinkable happens, we search for someone to blame. We forget that sometimes things just happen…and life goes on.

I loved giving these two the happy ending they both deserved, in God's time, and I fell in love with those two little boys! And when Gracie Jayne came walking in the door of that clinic, I knew she'd want Julia to have that baby, because Julia saw her for what she was: a mother doing her best to care for her child.

I love to create stories of family love and rejoicing, but we know parenting and marriage both require faith, hope, love and work. May God bless our families with all four!

I love to hear from readers. You can email me at loganherne@gmail.com, visit me at http://ruthloganherne.com and pray and chat with me anytime on Facebook! Or snail mail me at Love Inspired Books, 233 Broadway, Suite 1001, New York, NY 10279.

And thank you so much for taking the time to read Julia and Tanner's story. I'm so grateful!

Ruthy

LARGER-PRINT BOOKS!

GET 2 FREE LARGER-PRINT NOVELS PLUS 2 FREE MYSTERY GIFTS

Love Inspired®

SUSPENSE
RIVETING INSPIRATIONAL ROMANCE

Larger-print novels are now available...

LISLP15